I0591561

Murder on the Rerun

A Comedy-Mystery in Two Acts

Fred Carmichael

A SAMUEL FRENCH ACTING EDITION

FOUNDED 1830

SAMUELFRENCH.COM
SAMUELFRENCH-LONDON.CO.UK

FOR PRODUCTION ENQUIRIES

UNITED STATES AND CANADA
Info@SamuelFrench.com
1-866-598-8449

UNITED KINGDOM AND EUROPE
Theatre@SamuelFrench-London.co.uk
020-7255-4302

Each title is subject to availability from Samuel French, depending upon country of performance. Please be aware that *MURDER ON THE RERUN* may not be licensed by Samuel French in your territory. Professional and amateur producers should contact the nearest Samuel French office or licensing partner to verify availability.

Please refer to page 89 for further copyright information.

CAST

The action of the play takes place in a ski lodge in Northern Vermont.

ACT ONE

The present.

ACT TWO

A few hours later.

Murder on the Rerun

ACT ONE

SET: *The action of the play takes place in a modern ski lodge in the north of Vermont. Down right is an archway which leads off to the outside door and to the kitchen and dining room. Upstage of this is a jog in the wall and then parallel to the archway is a closet door. Above this is a right angle window with half the window on the right wall and half on the upstage wall. The window has no panes and looks out mostly on the sky or perhaps a tree-top as the lodge is on high elevation. Below the windows, on both walls, low shelves are built. The wall continues center where there is a staircase with the stairs coming down into the room. At the top of the stairs there is a landing and the passageway to the upstairs leading off to the left. Along the landing there is a railing leading to the rest of the upstage wall. Below the wall is a built-in bar containing all glasses, bottles, etc. necessary. There are two stools at the bar. The back wall slants to the left wall which contains a door opening offstage to the library. The furniture consists of a unit stage right which is a sectional sofa with the long part running parallel to the upstage wall and a smaller unit to its right so the sofa can sit three on the main part and one on the right side part. A large coffee table is in front of the unit. Stage left there is a chair with a matching hassock in front of it, a small end table to its left. The entire set is very sterile and modern with horizontal lines and as much glass and chrome as possi-*

5

ble. It does not look lived in but more like a rich
man's retreat which it is.
The Curtain opens in a blackout. There is a scream and
the sound of a fall.

HUGH. Who was that?

BETSY. What happened?

HUGH. Someone's hurt.

VALERIE. Nonsense, darling, that was acting.

EDWINA. No, it was real.

JUSTIN. It came from down here.

VALERIE. (*during above*) Someone found Jane, that's all.

BETSY. I'm scared.

HUGH. It's all right, Betsy.

EDWINA. (*during above*) Someone's hurt.

JUSTIN. Where the hell are the lights?

HUGH. Jane! Jane, are you all right?

JUSTIN. (*during above*) The light switch is here somewhere.

VALERIE. Jane's a writer. She's probably getting our reactions.

JUSTIN. I found the lights.

(*The lights come on to reveal JANE ACKERLY lying*
on the stairs with her head down as if she had
fallen. She is faced away from the audience. The
others are around her. JUSTIN WILLS is at the
light switch to the right of the stairs. He is mid-
dleaged and always tries to be the leader. VALERIE
VICKERS is on the landing. She is of indeterminate
age since her make-up and face lifts have been
perfect. She has fought for what she wants and is
not about to let go. HUGH LAWTON is by the

library door. He is same age as the others, hand-some, trying to be debonair, but at heart there is a strain of weakness. EDWINA DUNBAR is by the bar. She is an opportunist and out exclusively for herself. She is not as well put together as the others but is of approximately the same age. BETSY RANDOLPH is above the sofa. She is the youngest of the group and very pretty. At first meeting, one always thinks she is Hollywood's idea of the perfect ingenue. They are all well-dressed in expensive clothes for a winter weekend in Vermont.)

HUGH. (*crosses to* L. *of stairs and kneels beside* JANE) Jane. Darling.

BETSY. (*moves in*) Call someone. A doctor, Some-one.

EDWINA. Get a wet cloth.

JUSTIN. (*between BETSY and stairs*) Brandy.

BETSY. A doctor!

VALERIE. (*comes down one step*) Rescue squad, dar-ling. This is the country. They have rescue squads.

EDWINA. The back of her head, it's cut.

HUGH. She's not breathing.

JUSTIN. A pulse. Look for a pulse.

HUGH. I'm trying.

VALERIE. Just find her pulse, darling. Don't take ad-vantage of the poor child.

EDWINA. Does anyone know first aid?

VALERIE. I can do mouth-to-mouth resuscitation.

EDWINA. So I've heard.

HUGH. (*stands*) No. She's dead. Jane is dead.

JUSTIN. Oh, my God!

VALERIE. She can't be. She's just faking. (*starts for her*)

HUGH. No, she's dead.

BETSY. But who—why?

EDWINA. The dark. In the dark.

VALERIE. I said it was a stupid game.

JUSTIN. Tripped. She was at the top of the stairs and she tripped.

(*JANE stands up. We can now see she is in a dress with long sleeves. She is a pretty woman probably in her thirties. She is obviously dead as she wears a grey "Blithe Spirit" make-up covering her face and hands; however, this has not stopped an application of lipstick, rouge, mascara and whatever else enhances her appearance. JANE is an attractive woman, rather more of the outdoor type than the others.*)

JANE. (*The others keep looking at where she was lying as they cannot see the ghost of her.*) Tripped, hell! I was pushed! I've been murdered!

VALERIE. (*as they continue looking at where JANE was*) Accidents will happen.

JANE. (*crosses away* R.) It was no accident. I was pushed.

JUSTIN. (*starts for library*) I'd better call the police.

EDWINA. (*gets there before him and goes into the library*) Not before I call the paper. This is front page.

JANE. This is murder, I tell you.

BETSY. (*looks after EDWINA*) How can she be so heartless?

VALERIE. Easily. She's a newspaperwoman first and a human being second.

JANE. Doesn't anyone see me? Can't you hear me? I was murdered.

(*KITTY enters from down* R. *She is usually a happy soul and is bright and cheerful. She is wearing a rather nondescript dress and carries a book, the cover reading "Rules" and there are several loose pages showing.*)

KITTY. Hold it right there. None of you move. (*The others, beside JANE, freeze as they are.*)

JANE. (*goes to her*) Who are you?

KITTY. One thing at a time. (*talks directly to the audience*) Were you paying attention? That's the way it started. An accident, they said, but, of course, Jane knows better.

JANE. You're damned right I do.

KITTY. Don't get so excited.

JANE. Excited? Do you know what it's like to be murdered?

KITTY. I know what it's like to die violently.

JANE. Oh.

KITTY. But that was over two hundred years ago.

JANE. I don't—

KITTY. I can't talk to you now. You're getting me all out of sync. I'm just telling them what happened. (*indicates audience*) You go back up there and wait to be called. Your visa hasn't come through yet.

JANE. All this red tape. It's worse than an IRS audit.

KITTY. Go!

JANE. All right, I'm going. I'm going. (*She goes off down right sulking.*)

KITTY. (*to audience*) You'll have to forgive her. It's very traumatic being murdered. (*notices the others still frozen in position*) Oh, we don't need them any more right now. (*goes to right of sofa*) You can back where you were.

JUSTIN. (*As they unfreeze and look bewildered, ED-WINA comes in.*) What are we doing here?

KITTY. I called you so we could flashback to the night Jane died.

EDWINA. And I got that wonderful headline, "Author Trips, Hollywood Flips".

HUGH. (*moves down*) But this happened three years ago. What are we doing here now?

BETSY. It's a reenactment, isn't it?

KITTY. That's right. I have a sort of celestial VCR.

VALERIE. And we're in a freeze-frame.

KITTY. That's right. Time stood still. Now you can go back to what you were doing.

JUSTIN. You can do that?

KITTY. Time's so relative once you're up there.

EDWINA. You mean you're from — (*points upward*)

KITTY. Let's just call it "up there".

EDWINA. Amazing.

KITTY. All right, you return to what you were doing.

VALERIE. (*goes upstairs*) Good. I can remember very well what I was doing but for the life of me I can't remember who I was doing it with. (*exits*)

JUSTIN. (*goes down* R.) I was having a fight on the set. That damned star won't let me photograph the right side of her face. (*exits*)

HUGH. (*takes BETSY's hand as they go down* R.) Come on, Betsy, back to the studio commissary.

BETSY. How can I finish my diet salad after reliving this?

KITTY. You won't even remember it happened. (*HUGH and BETSY exit.*)

EDWINA. (*goes down center*) Don't send me back. We'll make a deal. Give me an interview and I'll split with you sixty-forty.

KITTY. (*goes to her*) Money's no good up there. Everything's free.

EDWINA. But what a story—"Proof of Life After Death".

KITTY. That's in The Inquirer once a month. Off with you.

EDWINA. (*goes down right*) Back to the mundane. (*to audience*) But you people never get tired reading about it, do you? Marriage, divorce, rape, drugs—all the little niceties of our life give you such a vicarious thrill. Keep reading. (*exits*)

KITTY. (*looks out front*) I bet you're really confused, right? (*goes down* C.) It's not my fault you wandered in here but, since you did, you might as well stay and see what happens. You saw Jane Ackerly die right there on the stairs. That was three years ago tonight. She floated up to us making a terrible fuss saying she was hit on the head and pushed. (*looks around a moment*) Will you excuse me a minute. (*gets a small dish of snacks from the bar and leaves her book there*) Whenever I get down here I'm so famished. I can't help it, I love snacks and junk food. They feed us, of course, but it's so nutritional. (*sits on the bar stool as she eats and talks*) Anyway, the bosses gave Jane all the usual forms for a return visit. No one thought she'd get a passport but it came through this morning with one hitch. Me! (*eats*) Umm, these are almost sinful. If I help Jane find her murderer, I knock off my last seventy-five demerits. I had over three thousand against me when I got there. Three thousand. Oh, I was a naughty girl, but they took pity on me up there. I looked so pitiful standing there looking through those gates like the Little Match Girl. But I'll get through them yet. (*holds out the book*) This is my rule book. (*goes down* C.) It's full of dos and don'ts. It tells me how to call people back, relive scenes, and all that. I'm working up to tonight when we gather all the suspects here (*goes down* L. *and looks up at room*) in the living room for the anniversary of Jane's death. Do you like this place? It's too modern for me but it's what those rich skiers like. It's owned by one Stanzio Garelli. He's a big film producer and this is his rustic hideaway in the Vermont mountains. (*goes up* C.) Some hideaway, over three hundred thousand dollars. I don't know why people can't just find a hill and ski down it. (*goes down* C.) Why do they have to be pulled up the mountain on a machine? None of the people you saw here ski of course but they've got the biggest après-ski wardrobe this side of Bloomingdale's. Did you figure out who they all were? I'll bring them back and introduce you. (*sits on the sofa and looks in her book*) Let's see. "Call Backs". C-C-C, there are so damned many rules. Here were are. That's simple. Now, hang on a minute. (*stands leaving the book on the sofa, closes eyes and stamps foot three times*)

JUSTIN. (*enters down* R.) Why do you keep calling me off the set?

KITTY. (*looks front*) It worked!

JUSTIN. I'm over-budget already.

KITTY. This is Justin Wills. He's a movie director.

JUSTIN. They know that. Everyone knows me. I'm a household word.

KITTY. So is Listerine or Pampers.

JUSTIN. You can talk. You're dead. I'm still down here trying to make a living. (*goes down* C. *and talks to the audience*) I didn't get where I am by luck, you know. I started as a messenger with the studio and worked my way up through assistant director until I finally got handed a cheapie no one else wanted. I turned that into a cult film. Then I got THE LOVES OF LAURA and —

KITTY. (*front*) Hang onto that. THE LOVES OF LAURA. It's an important clue.

JUSTIN. It got me an Academy Award and the envy of every two-bit director in Hollywood. Now I'm in trouble with a thirty million dollar fiasco and my career's on the line so can I go back now?

KITTY. They'll wait for you. Time is at a standstill.

JUSTIN. Time may be but my budget isn't.

KITTY. You're filming a nude scene, aren't you?

JUSTIN. The horse is nude, the star is in a bikini. (*turns to go and bumps into EDWINA as she enters*) Edwina, darling, how nice you look.

EDWINA. I know.

JUSTIN. I knew you did. (*They both smile at each other fatuously.*)

KITTY. (*front*) They're such good friends.

EDWINA. I hear your picture's in trouble.

JUSTIN. Nothing I can't solve if this interfering angel will —

KITTY. I'm no angel, just an apprentice trying to get through the gates.

EDWINA. I'm trying to get an interview in depth, something about clouds and harps.

KITTY. How little you know.

JUSTIN. (*to KITTY*) You're sure Edwina won't remember any of this?

KITTY. Positive.

JUSTIN. (*goes below EDWINA to down right*) Good, then I can tell her what I really think of her. (*turns and smiles at EDWINA*) Edwina, you are an egotistical, stupid, conniving — er — er

KITTY. Petty?

JUSTIN. Thank you. Petty, insincere little weasel of a woman. (*exits*)

EDWINA. Sometimes I think he doesn't like me.

KITTY. (*front*) This is Edwina—

EDWINA. (*front*) Edwina Dunbar, of course. The columnist. You've read me. I know, and seen me. The Tonight Show, Good Morning, America. You can't avoid me.

KITTY. Many have tried, few have succeeded.

EDWINA. You're sweet, you know that. You're really very sweet.

KITTY. That's all. You can go back now. We'll see you later.

EDWINA. You're going to interrupt me again?

KITTY. We're meeting here again in the present time.

EDWINA. Here at Stanzio's ski lodge?

KITTY. Yes, everyone who was here when Jane died.

EDWINA. I can't wait. None of us trusts the others, me included. It should be a most interesting meeting. (*to audience*) Are they coming, too?

KITTY. (*gets her book and returns it to shelves*) Of course.

EDWINA. (*front*) Don't you loathe these modern places? Makes me feel like I'm in the ladies room at the Guggenheim.

KITTY. (*comes down to sofa and sits on its back*) Miss Dunbar's a gossip columnist.

EDWINA. The best. (*front*) It's not what I write, you know. It's what I don't write that makes me a success. If I hadn't been with my publisher that night they picked him up for driving DWI, I'd probably still be reviewing flower shows. (*moves down* C.) I grabbed his little bag of dope from him and, would you believe it, I flushed it down the john at the police station with only the attendant watching me. (*moves down right*) She's on my payroll now, of course. She's also a witness and my insurance that I keep my job. (*steps down, intimately*)

Please don't believe everything you read about life in the fast lane. (*crosses to archway and turns back*) Only about ninety percent of it is true. (*exits*)

KITTY. That one's going to have a tough time getting through the gates up there. There's no one to blackmail, they're all so goody-goody. (*goes to shelves where she picks up a piece of fruit*) It sounds boring, doesn't it, but, you know, I'm getting used to it and I rather enjoy it now. (*tries to bite into apple*) Wax! If they'd had that in the Garden of Eden it would have saved a lot of trouble. (*puts apple back and goes* C.) It's time Jane got here, I hope they're sending her first class. (*A small scream, a thump, and the jangling of coat hangers comes from the closet.*) No, they didn't.

JANE. (*offstage in closet*) Help! I'm trapped!

KITTY. (*looks up*) This is no way to treat a heroine. (*opens closet door*) Hang on. I'll help you out.

JANE. (*She is on the floor of the closet with a coat and a hanger over her.*) This room's so small. Something's smothering me.

KITTY. Just some coats. There we are. (*JANE comes out. She is now wearing a long, flowing grey dress.*)

JANE. I was afraid they'd put me in solitary.

KITTY. Sometimes they have an odd sense of humor. (*hangs up the coat*)

JANE. I recognize that coat. It's Betsy's.

KITTY. That's right. She was here the night you were killed.

JANE. Here? (*looks around, goes to stairs*) I'm in Stanzio Garelli's ski lodge. This is where it happened. These are the stairs. This is where I was lying a minute ago.

KITTY. Three years to be exact.

JANE. Three years? But—

KITTY. (*closes closet door*) Don't forget about time. It's different up there. (*moves below sofa*) I still get confused. Einstein was trying to explain it to me again the other millenium.

JANE. Who are you? (*goes to her*) No, don't tell me. You're Kitty-something-or-other. I've seen you in the waiting room comparing notes with that snobbish Madame DuBarry.

KITTY. A misunderstood child. She's been waiting longer than I have.

JANE. Why do you have such a pink complexion? I look so ghostly.

KITTY. (*sits on sofa*) That fades in time.

JANE. (*sits sofa* C.) I hope so. All I've done in three years is fill out forms. In triplicate.

KITTY. You must have done it right because here you are.

JANE. I had a good case. Shouldn't I be allowed to find out who killed me?

KITTY. You didn't deserve to die so young.

JANE. I don't mind. I didn't know it would be so pleasant up there. Norman Vincent Peale was right.

KITTY. I felt the same way after I was shot.

JANE. Gangsters?

KITTY. No. I was a camp follower at Valley Forge and I followed too close.

JANE. But you don't have any wings.

KITTY. (*rises and goes to shelves for book*) I'm working towards them. If I can help you find your murderer they'll open those gates and I'll go right in.

JANE. I hope you make it.

KITTY. (*leans over back of sofa to JANE as she pulls out a form from the book*) Your application said that you want to get all the suspects together and see how they react.

JANE. That's what Agatha Christie suggested. I was having tea with her and she said gather all the suspects into the living room so that's what I put down. (*points to it on application*)

KITTY. And that's what you've been granted. (*puts book on table L. of chair*) They're all meeting here tonight and none of them knows the other is coming. I did that. Isn't it delicious? (*goes to bar and takes a nibble*)

JANE. How'd you manage it?

KITTY. I left messages on their service or with their agents saying Stanzio Garelli wanted to see them here alone on a very important matter.

JANE. (*laughs*) They all think it's a job. When Stanzio calls people run.

KITTY. He's that important?

JANE. He produced the top grossing pictures for the past five years. You don't get more important that that. I was hoping he'd do my new one but I died too soon.

KITTY. He produced it all right.

JANE. THE LOVES OF LAURA? How did he get hold of it?

KITTY. Ah, there's the rub as Shakespeare keeps mumbling.

JANE. (*rises and goes to KITTY*) No one had seen the script. I had it with me upstairs there the night I was pushed. Hugh. Did Hugh find it and give it to Stanzio?

KITTY. (*picks up book*) Let's hope we find out.

JANE. And I really won an Oscar for Best Writer?

KITTY. Not by name. It was awarded to Anonymous.

JANE. They couldn't have. It's not in the by-laws.

KITTY. (*puts book on shelves*) No one knew who wrote it. It caused a sensation.

JANE. (*to audience*) I wrote it! Did you hear? I wrote THE LOVES OF LAURA and — (*to KITTY*) What are all those people doing out there?

KITTY. (*goes above sofa*) Watching. They're going to stay right through till we find out who killed you. (*goes to bar*)

JANE. (*front*) I did write that script. That was my seventh produced. They were all good but THE LOVES OF LAURA was my crowning achievement. But did I get an Oscar? No. Instead I got a hit on the head. (*looks up*) It's all your fault. I understand I wasn't due till the turn of the century.

KITTY. (*moves down*) Don't blame them. Sometimes folks down here get carried away and take matters into their own hands. You have no idea how angry they get when there's a war. All the bookkeepers load up on overtime.

JANE. I can't believe it. I won an Oscar and I never got to deliver my acceptance speech.

KITTY. (*holds out dish to JANE*) Have some junk food. It will settle your nerves.

JANE. I have to watch my figure.

KITTY. Nonsense. Once you're through the gates everyone has a 36-25-36.

BETSY. (*offstage down* R.) Who wants me? Who called?

KITTY. Ah, there's Betsy Randolph. I've called them from sometime last week so the folks can meet them.

JANE. (*heads for closet*) I'll go back in the closet.

KITTY. She won't see you. You're not as advanced as I am.

JANE. That's good. Poor Betsy would burst into tears.

KITTY. (*calls*) Miss Randolph, in here.

BETSY. (*comes in to below sofa*) I was in the middle of giving my recipe for banana nut bread to the nicest interviewer from PEOPLE magazine and suddenly I'm here.

KITTY. It'll only take a minute.

BETSY. I hope so. I'm up to puréeing the bananas.

KITTY. I wish you'd brought some.

BETSY. It's too squishy.

KITTY. I want to introduce you to these nice people.

BETSY. (*steps down*) How do you do. Is this some committee meeting I forgot?

JANE. Always doing good works. Humane society, UNICEF, unwed fathers.

KITTY. (*goes to BETSY's* L.) We're all going to Stanzio Garelli's ski lodge in a few minutes and I want them to know who you are.

BETSY. Didn't they see THE LOVES OF LAURA?

JANE. (*to BETSY's* R.) Betsy was in it, too?

BETSY. (*front*) That was my first important role.

KITTY. (*sits on hassock*) Some of them may not go to the movies.

BETSY. You really should. It's our national art. (*to KITTY*) Do we have to go back to Stanzio's? I always hate it, all modern and sterile like a science fiction movie. Shouldn't a ski lodge be all logs and chintz?

JANE. You're thinking of Abe Lincoln.

BETSY. (*goes below stairs*) And Stanzio's is where Jane fell down.

JANE. (*goes above sofa to BETSY*) Where I was pushed.

KITTY. (*settles back in chair*) You can't get out of it. You won't remember any of this and you'll have a very plausible reason for showing up.

BETSY. It all sounds dreadfully morbid. (*goes* D.C. *to audience*) A professional ingenue shouldn't have to go through these scenes. I never wanted to be an actress. My boyfriend entered me in a beauty contest. I won first prize as Miss Pizza Topping of Rochester, New York. (*goes below sofa*) Like all beauty queens, I went to Hollywood, but I'm still a litte girl at heart who likes to play tennis and cook and thinks America is just a cottage with a picket fence and Mom's apple pie. (*goes to arch* D.R., *turns back*) Of course now that I'm a success I have my apple pie a la mode. (*exits*)

KITTY. (*goes to shelves for her book*) I wonder if I can't think up pie and ice cream.

JANE. I'm delighted Betsy got into THE LOVES OF LAURA. Hugh discovered her, you know. It was at a Drive-In and she served him his double cheeseburger and fries on roller skates.

KITTY. (*brings book to back of sofa*) Double cheeseburgers —

JANE. (*moves to her*) Betsy came to help Hugh's secretary. She organized his fan club in Japan. I always said she was responsible for his getting more fan mail than Godzilla. Hugh even got her an agent.

KITTY. Nothing under pie. How about cheeseburgers?

JANE. Hugh always helps people. Me for example. (*gives up getting her attention, goes* D.C. *and talks to the audience*) My second book was ADVENTURE IN HONDURAS and Stanzio Garelli bought it from the proofs and hired me to do the script. I'd found my place in life. I had a script mind. I was good at it. I wrote another and Hugh had the lead. We had conferences over line changes he wanted and then we had conferences without discussing the script and, before I knew it, we were married. Then I wrote THE LOVES OF

LAURA. Maybe it's best I died because I could never top that one.

KITTY. Damn! (*reads*) "No food ordered unless essential to your work." (*closes book*)

VALERIE. (*comes storming in at the top of the stairs*) Why do you keep interrupting me? Is nothing sacred?

JANE. (*Front; she sits in chair.*) Hold onto your husbands. Here's Valerie.

KITTY. I want these nice people to know who you are.

VALERIE. (*crosses down stairs*) Everyone knows Valerie Vickers. I've been a star since — well, since I was a teenager.

KITTY. Five husbands and thirty-two movies later and you're still a star.

VALERIE. Thirty-one movies.

KITTY. Aren't you forgetting STAG PARTY SENSATION?

VALERIE. (*goes to KITTY*) Oh, my God, you won't tell Edwina, will you?

KITTY. (*puts book on shelves*) I'm not a tattle-tale.

VALERIE. I was a mere child. I thought STAG PARTY SENSATION was about a deer. You know, like Bambi. (*comes down to* R. *of sofa*)

JANE. Oh, come now —

VALERIE. Besides, I wasn't Valerie Vickers then. I was little Emily Pyle, from East Scranton. (*gets carried away with her performance, crosses* D.C.) Oh, where is that innocent child now?

JANE. Here she goes!

VALERIE. Where is that sweet girl who used to go to the park and play with the squirrels and chipmunks?

HUGH. (*starts applauding offstage down* R. *as he enters*) You're giving one of your best performances, Valerie.

JANE. (*rises*) Hugh. My Hugh.

VALERIE. (*breaking her mood*) I didn't know you were going to be here.

HUGH. Neither did I.

JANE. You look marvelous.

KITTY. (*goes below sofa*) I called you here to meet these nice people.

HUGH. (*front*) Ah, my fans. How do you do.

KITTY. This is just an introductory meeting which you will forget as soon as it's over.

JANE. It's like group therapy.

VALERIE. You mean we're letting our hair down?

HUGH. You can take yours off. I know it's a wig.

VALERIE. (*steps down to audience*) I don't want you to get the wrong idea about me. That little bit about the sweet girl with the chipmunks? That's my image. I created it and I cultivated it. What was I supposed to do with my life, be a secretary from nine to five? Not me. I worked my way up from the chorus to a seven year contract with M-G-M. I did whatever and whoever I could to get ahead. I'm a movie star twenty-four hours a day. That's my job and I'm damn good at it. (*goes down right*) I've sacrificed a lot for my showplace in Beverly Hills, my swimming pool, and my Ferrari, but what secretary has that? Do you blame me for what I am? Think it over. Maybe you'll find you're just a little bit jealous. (*exits*)

HUGH. Poor thing. She never got over missing the Oscar for THE LOVES OF LAURA.

JANE. Was she nominated? (*KITTY nods her head.*)

HUGH. I thought it was very generous of me to include her in my acceptance speech.

JANE. (*comes close to HUGH*) Hugh won? I'm so glad.

HUGH. (*front*) I'm delighted to meet you. Is there some award you want to present?

JANE. One kiss. Just one little kiss.

KITTY. I wanted these folks to see you before we go to Stanzio's.

JANE. Not a passionate one.

HUGH. I'm not going there.

JANE. Just one little peck.

KITTY. Oh, yes you are.

HUGH. (*as JANE kisses his cheek, reacts with a yelp and goes D.R.*) Ow! It's that damned shaving cream. I've got razor burn again.

JANE. (*sinks on hassock*) I tried.

KITTY. (*sits on sofa*) You can go. I'll call you back later.

HUGH. We'll see about that. (*front*) Thanks for coming. It's you fans who made me a star. You and, of course, my talent. I love you all, each and everyone of you. (*starts to exit and turns back*) Not the men, of course. I'm fond of you men. But the ladies—ah, I just love you ladies. (*blows a kiss and exits*)

KITTY. You married that?

JANE. I know he sounds conceited, but why shouldn't he be? I'm sure while I was at my IBM Selectric he was charming some cute little script girl but it's all in fun.

KITTY. Some fun. I could show you—(*rises and goes to bar*) No, that's mean.

JANE. (*goes to KITTY's L. at bar*) Show me what?

KITTY. (*picks up dish of snacks*) No, you keep your illusions.

JANE. About what? Hugh? What illusions?

KITTY. (*eating as she moves away R.*) Nothing, nothing, nothing.

JANE. He didn't kill me. He couldn't have.

KITTY. No, he was a faithful husband and — (*lurches forward as if hit*) Ow! (*looks up*) What did you do that for?

JANE. What? What happened?

KITTY. They hit me.

JANE. We don't have corporal punishment up there, do we?

KITTY. (*looks in book on shelves*) Let me look it up.

JANE. (*goes* U.C.) I guess once you get past the gates it's all right, beautiful music and such?

KITTY. That's the gossip. (*in book*) Here it is. (*reads*) "Corporal punishment is permissable. One can slap a worker when he tells a fib."

JANE. All you said was Hugh was faithful and — that was a lie? (*crosses to center of chair*) I don't believe it. I absolutely don't believe it.

KITTY. (*goes above sofa*) You want proof?

JANE. (*confused, goes towards library*) No! Yes! I don't know.

KITTY. You remember the night you were murdered?

JANE. Vividly.

KITTY. (*puts the snack dish on the bar*) You were worried Hugh would be suicidal with despair?

JANE. The poor dear. He loved me so.

KITTY. (*goes to the* R. *of stairs*) That night, after the local police had finished their investigation and Edwina had called in the story, Hugh came downstairs to get a drink. (*HUGH comes down and goes to bar.*)

JANE. Scotch on the rocks. Johnny Walker Red. (*She goes to him as he pours drink.*) Look at him, Kitty, he's finding solace in the bottle. He's desolate. Oh, he'll never recover from this. I told you, he's destroyed.

KITTY. (*goes to HUGH's* R.) Actually, he's wondering what photo of him they'll use in the papers.

HUGH. (*musing*) I hope they use that one from ADVENTURE IN HONDURAS.

JANE. He's just keeping his mind off the tragedy.

KITTY. (*not believing this*) Uh-huh.

JANE. I wish I could comfort him. (*to him as he drinks*) Hugh, dear, it's all right. I don't seem to mind being dead.

KITTY. He can't hear you. (*HUGH goes below sofa.*)

JANE. Perhaps the thought gets through.

HUGH. I must play that part in THE LOVES OF LAURA. (*BETSY comes downstairs.*)

KITTY. Well, what do you know? Here comes Miss Apple Pie.

JANE. She'll comfort him.

BETSY. Hugh.

HUGH. Betsy.

KITTY. (*goes to R. of sofa*) That's some comfort.

JANE. She'll know how to relax him.

BETSY. (*goes to HUGH*) Everyone's gone to bed.

HUGH. Watch out for Edwina. She's always snooping.

BETSY. She's taking her Estee Lauder bubble bath.

HUGH. You're sure we're alone?

BETSY. Positive. (*They go into a deep and passionate embrace.*)

JANE. Look at that! Do you see what he's doing?

KITTY. (*by sofa R., goes close to watch them*) I don't think she's relaxing him very much.

JANE. (*goes D.C., to HUGH*) Stop it this instant! Hugh, I'm here. I'm watching. I'm not even cold in the ground.

KITTY. And he's getting hot up here.

JANE. (*to KITTY*) Can't you stop them?

KITTY. I'm rather enjoying it. I can barely remember

how nice it was. (*BETSY and HUGH sink onto the sofa in an embrace.*) When I think of the men I seduced. There was that lieutenant — (*reacts as if slapped again*) Ow! (*looks up*) Sorry! (*to JANE*) They don't like that kind of talk.

HUGH. (*breaks the kiss*) Not now. Edwina may come down.

BETSY. (*giggles*) Swathed only in bubbles.

HUGH. If she knew about us it would ruin me.

BETSY. Now we can tell everyone.

HUGH. There has to be a suitable mourning period.

KITTY. He must mean more than two hours.

BETSY. Why don't you throw yourself on her casket?

HUGH. That's always good for the front page of the Daily News.

JANE. I hope you get splinters in your —

KITTY. We must think kind thoughts.

HUGH. We can start being seen together in six months.

BETSY. And announce our engagement at a large press party at the Hilton.

JANE. (*pacing indignantly*) I don't believe it. Right under my very nose.

HUGH. This is much better than divorcing. That's such rotten publicity.

JANE. It didn't hurt that Taylor girl.

BETSY. Now we can be together always. (*They kiss.*)

KITTY. (*goes to JANE*) And you really thought you two were America's Sweethearts?

JANE. We had a six page spread in Good Housekeeping, Barbara Walters interviewed us and once we were even mentioned by Billy Graham. (*sits on hassock*) I think I'm going to cry.

KITTY. You can't. We don't have tears.

JANE. (*notices BETSY rubbing HUGH's head and*

messing his hair) He hates to have his hair mussed.

HUGH. (*straightens up*) Don't muss my hair.

BETSY. No one's watching.

HUGH. You never know.

JANE. You're damned right you don't.

BETSY. After the funeral, can't we sneak away somewhere? Hawaii? Acapulco?

HUGH. I know this little place outside Manzanillo— (*pronounced Mon-zan-ee-yo*)

JANE. (*rises*) That's where we spent our honeymoon.

BETSY. Just the two of us, alone. Unless we're working, of course.

HUGH. Maybe Jane's new script.

BETSY. She said it was very good.

JANE. (*moves above sofa*) It was terrific.

BETSY. What's it called?

HUGH and JANE. THE LOVES OF LAURA.

BETSY. Is it really good?

HUGH. How would I know? She never shows— showed—me anything before it was finished.

BETSY. When you find it, you will let me see it, won't you?

HUGH. Of course.

BETSY. Maybe it has leads for the two of us. We'll set the town on its ear. Just us. You and me. (*kisses him*)

JANE. (*moves to KITTY*) I am furious. I typed my fingers to the knuckle for that?

KITTY. Think how mad you'd be if you wrote longhand.

JANE. (*sits in the chair sulking*) Haven't we had enough of this? I'd rather watch a rerun of LASSIE.

KITTY. Whatever you want. I'm here to help. (*moves to C. of sofa, claps hands*) All right, you two. Break it up. Break it up!

BETSY. (*as they break the kiss*) What—who said that?

HUGH. Edwina. It's Edwina.

KITTY. No, it's just me again.

BETSY. I feel as if I'm on a casette.

HUGH. (*rises*) Why did we have to repeat this?

KITTY. Just a whim of mine. You two go back upstairs and you'll forget all about it.

BETSY. (*rises, takes HUGH's hand and takes him to the stairs*) Why don't you just go back and sit on a cloud?

JANE. (*to KITTY*) They don't understand, do they?

KITTY. (*moves above JANE*) Cloud-sitting would be a bore.

BETSY. (*as she and HUGH are on landing*) Then go to hell.

JANE. She's going the opposite way.

KITTY. You go to bed.

BETSY. That's what I intend to do, but not alone. (*takes HUGH off with her*)

JANE. (*rises and paces below sofa*) I am livid. I don't feel in the least bit angelic.

KITTY. Calm down.

JANE. How can I be calm? Where's that book? (*grabs the book from shelves and looks in the index*)

KITTY. (*goes to her*) What are you doing?

JANE. I'll take care of Hugh.

KITTY. What are you looking up?

JANE. How to make him do a musical version of PEER GYNT.

KITTY. (*takes book back*) We don't use this for revenge.

JANE. (*goes to bar as KITTY puts book on shelves; to audience*) Did you see them? Of course you did. I feel so naive. While I was slaving over a hot typewriter, Hugh was slaving over a hot ingenue.

KITTY. (*goes to JANE's* R., *to audience*) She's upset. You can understand that, can't you?

JANE. They both pushed me. Together. I was hit on the head and then I felt twenty fingers on my back and ten of them had long fingernails.

KITTY. (*guides her to bar*) You're making that up.

JANE. What am I going to do?

KITTY. Sit down here and count to ten.

JANE. I don't want —

KITTY. (*pushes her down on bar stool*) Count!

JANE. One, two, three, four —

KITTY. Have some snacks. Oh, they're all gone. (*puts dish down, picks up another*)

JANE. — five, six, seven, eight, nine, ten.

KITTY. Olives! (*eats one*) Here, Jane, have one.

JANE. Only if it's dunked in a martini.

KITTY. (*sits by her as she eats another olive*) I wish we had olives up there. The menu in the commissary is so limiting.

JANE. (*pulls herself together and rises*) I've come to a decision.

KITTY. That sounds ominous.

JANE. I want to go back. I don't care who killed me. (*goes* D.C.) I just want to get out of here.

KITTY. (*worried*) You can't.

JANE. I asked to come down, can't I ask to go back?

KITTY. What about me?

JANE. You can stay if you want to.

KITTY. (*rises and goes to JANE*) But this is my big chance. I've got to help you find your murderer. I've flopped so many times already.

JANE. On other cases?

KITTY. (*moves below chair*) I spent ages on that missing person case. I looked everywhere — in swamps, the bottom of muddy old lakes, and even in a garbage disposal unit and I couldn't find him.

JANE. Who?

KITTY. (*turns*) Jimmy Hoffa. Maybe he had plastic surgery and now he's Idi Amin.

JANE. (*sits on sofa*) You did your best.

KITTY. (*goes to her*) I've always been good at the little things.

JANE. Like what?

KITTY. (*moves* C.) Oh, sitting on people's shoulders and whispering like their conscience when they're about to sin. I've stopped more adultery than the Pope.

JANE. You should have been on Hugh's shoulder.

KITTY. I can't be everywhere at once. Sometimes I make people confess to their little indiscretions. They feel better and I get another demerit erased, (*sits by JANE*) but I'll never get through those gates without a big case and this was going to be it and now you want to go back and leave me and—(*leans on JANE's shoulder and is crying without tears*) Oh, I wish I could cry real tears.

JANE. (*patting her shoulder*) There, there, Kitty.

KITTY. I've always messed things up. Remember, I told you I was shot and killed at Valley Forge?

JANE. I remember.

KITTY. That isn't quite the truth. I died because I was greedy. General Washington threw that silver dollar across the Potomac and—

JANE. Yes.

KITTY. I was stooping down to pick it up when I fell in the river and drowned. (*wails*)

JANE. (*starts laughing*) You don't mean it? You picked up the—(*Laughter takes over.*)

KITTY. It doesn't help to have you laugh at me.

JANE. That's the most ridiculous thing I ever heard.

KITTY. It does seem rather silly, but at least I got you laughing. You feel better now, don't you?

JANE. Much.

KITTY. And you won't go back?

JANE. You win. I'll help you get your wings. Oh, dear, I sound like Uncle Sam talking to an air force recruit.

KITTY. You're nice. You're going to make a very respectable angel. (*goes to bar*) Now you'll have an olive?

JANE. No, thank you.

KITTY. (*takes one*) Wouldn't you think someone as rich as Mr. Garelli would have loads of tid-bits and munchies?

JANE. (*crosses KITTY*) What about THE LOVES OF LAURA? I had it with me the night — it happened. I'd told Stanzio I was bringing him the best writing since Moses walked down the mountain with those tablets.

KITTY. Careful, Jane. They're very touchy about things like that.

JANE. (*looks up*) I was only joking.

KITTY. You never did show the script to Mr. Garelli, did you?

JANE. (*goes to windows and looks out*) How could I? We were marooned in a blizzard and his plane was so delayed he missed the whole weekend.

KITTY. (*goes* C.) Skiers are miserable without enough snow because they can't ski and then they're miserable with too much snow because they can't get up the slopes. Why don't they just take up scuba-diving?

JANE. (*goes to her*) I had the script in my attaché case. (*goes to library*) That first night someone must have brought it down here, xeroxed it in the library, and taken it back without my knowing it.

KITTY. (*crosses by hassock*) Then whoever did that killed you?

JANE. But who? (*sits in chair*) Stanzio asks us here—five dear friends. That's Hollywood style, you know. We're dear friends who are so jealous of each other we could—

KITTY. Commit murder?

JANE. Obviously. But what happened to the script? Who took it to Stanzio and why was it anonymous?

KITTY. Would you like to see how that happened?

JANE. Curiosity killed the cat but I'm already dead so let me see it.

KITTY. (*gets book from shelves and brings it to above the sofa*) Let's see how to bring that about. (*to audience*) You don't mind waiting a bit longer for us to get to the present time, do you? It's only fair for Jane to see her group plotting away. (*from book*) Here we are. "Events taking place elsewhere."

JANE. (*goes to her*) Where are we going?

KITTY. A little bar in Ventura called Outtakes.

JANE. (*moves away* D.L.) That's a terrible joint.

KITTY. That's where the five of them plotted their course to the Oscars two months after you died. (*front and crosses* C.) Now you all use your imagination. You'll have to excuse me for being childish but this is what the books says. (*does the childish rhyme and gesture of PATTY-CAKE and yells*) Ventura. Outtakes Bar.

JANE. Are you sure that's how to do it?

KITTY. (*goes to her*) It must be because here they come. (*turns front*) Amazing, isn't it?

(*The five of them come in and gather around the coffee
    table. They come in unemotionally and sit as if at a*

banquette. BETSY sits D.R. *on the sofa with
HUGH above her, JUSTIN sits in the middle with
EDWINA to his left and VALERIE to the* C.)

JANE. Where are they going?

KITTY. (*as they sit down*) This will serve as the table
they were sitting around. (*goes* C. *as they remain in
frozen positions*) Now you'll see what happened to your
script. Ready?

JANE. (*Watching the others, she goes below KITTY
and below sofa to* D.R.) I'm a little nervous.

KITTY. Go! (*As she gestures, they unfreeze and continue as if they had been drinking and talking.*)

JUSTIN. . . . and so we all admit we received a copy of
THE LOVES OF LAURA in the mail Wednesday
morning.

JANE. Where did they get them from?

EDWINA. And we've no idea who sent them?

HUGH. One of us obviously. We were the only people
at Stanzio's lodge when the script disappeared.

BETSY. You're absolutely sure Jane had it with her?

HUGH. Positive.

VALERIE. It's all she talked about at dinner,
remember?

JANE. (*goes above sofa*) Me and my big mouth.

BETSY. I can't believe one of us would steal it.

VALERIE. Why not? One of us stole her husband.

JANE. (*leans over VALERIE's shoulder*) Good for
you, Valerie.

BETSY. That's a terrible thing to say.

HUGH. (*at the same time*) Valerie!

VALERIE. Come on, Betsy. We all knew what was going on.

JANE. I didn't.

EDWINA. I suppressed the story in exchange for an exclusive with Hugh on the funeral, didn't I, dear?

HUGH. Edwina, you promised—

BETSY. (*turns on him*) Is that true?

HUGH. It would have started a lot of filthy rumors.

VALERIE. Where there's smoke—

KITTY. (*sits on hassock and leans in towards them*) This is exciting.

BETSY. Edwina, it's time someone told you off.

JUSTIN. (*rising above the growing fight*) Well, not now! We're here for business. You two can meet with pistols at dawn if you want, but right now we have our futures to think about.

VALERIE. (*applauds*) That's the director for you. Calm us down.

HUGH. Yes, Betsy, let's get on with it.

BETSY. You're a big help.

JANE. (*to KITTY*) He always collapsed in a crisis like a cold soufflé.

EDWINA. I accept your apology.

BETSY. I didn't apologize. (*JANE crosses by her.*)

EDWINA. (*smiles*) You will, dear. You will.

JANE. (*leans in over BETSY*) She means you'd better.

JUSTIN. To get back to THE LOVES OF LAURA. We know someone stole the script, read it, and realized Jane was right. It was brilliant. That person mailed us xeroxed copies with the stipulations attached.

JANE. (*goes to above JUSTIN*) What stipulations?

VALERIE. Thank God for that.

JANE. (*yelling in JUSTIN's ear*) I said, "What stipulations?"

JUSTIN. I am to direct the picture, Betsy plays Laura—

VALERIE. And I get Myra. It's a much better role.

BETSY. And much older.

EDWINA. The letter says I get an exclusive on everything connected with LAURA straight through the opening.

HUGH. But why was this all done, that's what I want to know?

JANE. (*moves towards KITTY*) Me, too.

KITTY. And me.

JUSTIN. Let's reconstruct the whole thing. Someone—

JANE. (*turns to them*) One of you—

EDWINA. One of us—

JUSTIN. Read the script of LAURA, realized how good it was and wanted to guarantee he participated in it.

VALERIE. Or she, darling. Don't forget the three of us.

BETSY. Why couldn't this person claim to have written the script? Who could tell?

HUGH. I could.

JUSTIN. How?

HUGH. There are certain moments, little snippets here and there from Jane's past only I knew about.

EDWINA. Then you can still prove it and you get the rights.

JUSTIN. The royalites all go into a numbered Swiss bank account.

HUGH. Perhaps I'm just being generous.

BETSY. The marriage contract. It said that—

HUGH. Why don't you shut up?

JANE. Good for Betsy.

BETSY. But we might as well be honest, Hugh.

KITTY. Why start now?

VALERIE. Why start now? (*KITTY and JANE exchange a nod.*)

EDWINA. So there was a marriage contract between you and Jane?

HUGH. Well—

BETSY. It's just like the one we have, isn't it?

JANE. (*looks to KITTY*) They have one?

EDWINA. Why, Hugh, a pre-marital contract doesn't sound like you expect the marriage to last.

JANE. They're married?

KITTY. Didn't you guess?

HUGH. My lawyer advised it.

EDWINA. Ah, the fly in the ointment. All Jane's effects didn't go to you, did they, Hugh?

JANE. No way.

HUGH. Everything except the community property went to that stupid university in the Midwest.

JUSTIN. They would have inherited the rights to THE LOVES OF LAURA.

VALERIE. Hugh is in the same boat as the rest of us.

JUSTIN. Whoever took the script sent it to Stanzio thereby guaranteeing his future in the picture.

JANE. (*moves above sofa*) But which of you?

VALERIE. But which of us?

EDWINA. The royalties go into the Swiss bank account which cannot be touched for five years until the tv, foreign, and casette rights are all in. One of us here is a lot smarter than I thought.

JANE. (*leans over EDWINA*) It could be you, Edwina.

VALERIE. It could be you, Edwina.

JANE. (*turns to VALERIE*) Stop repeating everything I say.

JUSTIN. Isn't it time we mention what's lurking in the back of all our minds?

HUGH. Which is?

JUSTIN. We played that stupid game of Sardine. We put the lights out and wandered around the lodge looking for who was it. We heard a scream and we found Jane dead.

VALERIE. We have total recall, darling.

JUSTIN. The coroner said the cut on her head came from the stairs but we all know it could have come from that objet d'art thing in the upstairs hall.

BETSY. Justin, what are you saying?

JUSTIN. Isn't that a blunt instrument?

JANE. (*rubs her head*) Blunt and hard.

JUSTIN. Wasn't Jane hit and then pushed to make it look like an accident? (*looks from one to the other*) It's what we're all thinking, isn't it?

JANE. Good for Justin.

EDWINA. It had crossed my mind.

VALERIE. But we're all such dear friends . . . aren't we?

BETSY. Murder? None of us could do that.

JUSTIN. Couldn't we? Just look at us. Have you ever seen a more greedy, avaricious group?

VALERIE. We're only trying to get ahead. It's the American way of life.

HUGH. But I hate to believe that one of us would—

VALERIE. It doesn't really matter, does it? Jane is gone. We can't bring her back.

KITTY. Would they want to? (*JANE goes towards KITTY.*)

JUSTIN. Yes. Jane is happy wherever she is.

JANE. At the moment, I am miserable.

BETSY. Poor Jane.

JANE. (*turns to them*) Stop calling me poor Jane. I died rich.

VALERIE. How do we know we can trust each other? Suppose one of us goes to the authorities. He'd be a national hero.

EDWINA. I somehow don't see you on Mount Rushmore.

VALERIE. How about little Goody-Twoshoes?

BETSY. It would ruin Hugh.

HUGH. Just lay off, Valerie.

VALERIE. (*rises angrily*) Don't tell me what to do. It's not my wife that was pushed downstairs. (*goes L. of coffee table*) That was very convenient, wasn't it?

JUSTIN. Aren't you just shifting the scene away from yourself, Valerie?

VALERIE. What about you? You seem to have taken charge. Your career hasn't been doing too well lately and—

JUSTIN. (*rises*) Stop it right there. We're all in this together and this back-biting will get us nowhere.

KITTY. It's exciting though.

JUSTIN. We all have a lot on the line. No one outside of the five of us need ever know what's happened. Stanzio says he will produce the movie and the script credit will read "By Anonymous".

JANE. I should contact the Dramatists Guild.

JUSTIN. Whether Jane fell or was pushed is immaterial.

JANE. To everyone but Jane.

JUSTIN. (*sits on sofa*) I suggest we all calm down and agree that we go ahead with the plan.

EDWINA. Well put, dear.

JUSTIN. As for myself, I'd like to congratulate whichever of us took advantage of this opportunity.

VALERIE. (*sits on sofa*) Are you just being self-congratulatory, darling?

JUSTIN. (*smiles at her*) You'll never know. Then are we all agreed? We go ahead as outlined?

HUGH. It's the only sensible thing to do.

JUSTIN. (*puts his hand out*) Agreed? (*They all put their hand on top of his.*)

ALL. Agreed.

KITTY. (*rises with a gesture*) Stop! Hold it right there! (*They freeze in position. To JANE:*) A nice group of friends you have.

JANE. (*as she goes above sofa looking closely at each one*) But which killed me? Valerie? She'd murder for a close-up. Justin? After three divorces, his community property is divided up like Gaul. Edwina? She'd kill her own mother to interview herself on death row. And Hugh? My dear, sweet husband who is a louse. (*to BETSY*) And let's not forget this one. Another Bonnie looking for a Clyde. (*moves away to windows*) Oh, get rid of them. Get them to the present. They look like a freeze-frame from ALL ABOUT EVE.

KITTY. (*to them, claps her hands*) O.K. Break it up. Back to wherever you were. (*They all exit silently with no communication, they go* D.R.) You'll be back here again in a few minutes.

JANE. (*goes above sofa with book*) Couldn't we call Sherlock Holmes?

KITTY. (*goes to her*) He's a character.

JANE. (*gives book to KITTY*) How about Dashiel Hammett or that gloomy little man who's always by himself in the corner of the waiting room?

KITTY. Edgar Allen Poe?

JANE. That's the one.

KITTY. All he ever does is mumble "Never more, quoth the raven, never more."

JANE. While sipping his Amontillado. (*They laugh as JANE goes to bar.*) How about looking in your book and reconstructing my death scene?

KITTY. They won't let us dabble in violence.

JANE. (*picks up bottle*) Oh, how I wish I wanted a double Scotch, but I haven't felt like a Happy Hour since I got up there. (*sits on* L. *stool*) Do you suppose

Alcoholics Anonymous is in charge of the waiting room?

KITTY. (*crosses and sits on* R. *stool*) Along with Weight Watchers and Smoke Enders.

JANE. I don't even want a cigarette and I wouldn't have to worry about the Surgeon General. It wouldn't be dangerous to my health. I'm already dead.

KITTY. (*looks in book*) Now to get to the present. I've arranged it for the third anniversary of your death in the place where it happened. They each think no one else has been invited. Hugh and Betsy came together, of course.

JANE. Of course.

KITTY. There's bound to be tension and fights and—

JANE. What if there isn't?

KITTY. I have a prop that will start things going. (*goes* U.C. *with book*) Here we are. The present. Oh, that's a snap. (*closes book and puts it on shelves, goes down by closet*) All I have to do is think and we get there.

JANE. (*sees KITTY standing there with her eyes closed*) Are you thinking or napping?

JANE. Shh! I'm thinking. Very hard. The present. The present.

VALERIE. (*Comes sweeping in* D.R., *she is wearing a fur coat, her head is swathed in a chiffon scarf and she wears sun glasses making her almost unrecognizable.*) Stan! Stanzio! (*crosses to foot of stairs*)

JANE. (*rises*) I thought they were here already.

VALERIE. (*looking up the stairs*) Where the hell are you?

KITTY. (*goes above the sofa to VALERIE*) I guess I'm not up to the present. (*behind her, calls to her*) Miss Vickers.

VALERIE. (*turns*) It's you again. Once and for all what are you doing?

KITTY. I'm trying to—

VALERIE. (*goes* D.C. *furious*) I get a message Stanzio wants to see me, I leave my shooting in Montreal, show up here in disguise and—(*unwraps the scarf and takes off sun glasses*)

KITTY. (*crosses above the sofa*) If you'll just—

VALERIE. You've got me rattling around in time like a disabled missile (*heads for archway* D.R.) and what's more you're bringing on one of my migraines.

KITTY. You can't go—(*gets between VALERIE and the archway*)

VALERIE. Get out of my way, you interfering—

KITTY. Stop! (*gestures and VALERIE freezes*)

JANE. (*goes* D.C.) Kitty, you're marvelous.

KITTY. It's nothing really.

JANE. (*walks to VALERIE, then looks front*) Wouldn't you love to do that when Congress is in session?

KITTY. I've got to think ahead a few more hours until they're all here. (*shuts eyes and thinks; gestures to VALERIE*) You go upstairs and wait till I catch up to you. (*VALERIE unfreezes and solemnly goes upstairs.*)

JANE. (*follows her to the foot of the stairs*) And she rushed here thinking Stanzio wanted to discuss that remake of SALOME. (*to VALERIE as she goes upstairs*) Did you know that dance wasn't bumps and grinds, just seven veils?

KITTY. (*opens eyes*) There. I think I've gotten us to the present.

JANE. (*goes to her*) What do I do? Just watch and listen and hope I catch a clue?

KITTY. I'll help all I can. I'd better get the coffee. (*starts for* D.R. *exit*)

JANE. What coffee?

KITTY. (*turns*) The coffee I'm serving after dinner.

I'm the maid. I thought it would be helpful if I was real to them so I said Mr. Garelli had hired me for the weekend. Isn't that clever?

JANE. You can do that?

KITTY. A snap. (*The others come downstairs and solemnly arrange themselves; JUSTIN sits in the chair, VALERIE is looking out the windows, BETSY is sitting on* C. *of sofa, HUGH is to her* R. *sitting, EDWINA is in the library on the phone.*) Here they come to get into position for where they are now.

JANE. Where's Edwina?

KITTY. In the library on the phone. I am so excited. Think of the maid's fringe benefits.

JANE. Like what?

KITTY. They let me have props up there if I'm real. Oh, the food I can order. (*as she exits*) Chocolate sundaes, cheesecake, double banana splits —

JANE. (*crosses* C. *as the others seat themselves*) If only you knew I was here. Which of you hit me? I never did like that little statue on the table upstairs. Stanzio claims he got it in Florence, but I knew he got it with Green Stamps. (*waits a moment, watching them still frozen*) Aren't you coming to life?

BETSY. (*As they all break into the present, EDWINA can be heard on the phone. It is only a mumbling and not distinct.*) I thought it was a remarkably good dinner. (*JANE sits at the bar.*)

JUSTIN. I was surprised that bucolic maid could even thaw food.

BETSY. What do you suppose Edwina is doing on that phone?

VALERIE. (*turns*) Increasing Stanzio's bill.

BETSY. She's making up some blind item for her column.

HUGH. She can twist nothing into something.

VALERIE. (*leans over HUGH*) Don't we know, darling. There's not one of us hasn't been burnt by her.

EDWINA. (*comes out of the library*) That was certainly a profitable call.

VALERIE. Did you spell my name right?

EDWINA. Stanzio is not coming.

JUSTIN. Of course he is. He asked us here, didn't he?

EDWINA. (*goes U.C.*) I have his private number in Pacific Palisades. His housekeeper said he left for London this morning.

HUGH. Then he's stopping here on the way.

EDWINA. He went via the Polar route.

JUSTIN. Is this some sort of practical joke?

JANE. Played by Kitty.

EDWINA. Interesting, isn't it?

JUSTIN. What?

EDWINA. The five of us who benefited from Jane's death are all gathered here by some hoax and you know what the date is, don't you?

JUSTIN. Three years ago tonight Jane died.

HUGH. I know.

JANE. Don't everyone weep.

BETSY. (*rises and goes D.R.*) I don't like it. I want to go. Come on, Hugh, let's get out of here.

HUGH. In this blizzard, from this hilltop? You're not a very good skier.

JANE. (*rises and looks out windows*) A blizzard? Good for Kitty.

JUSTIN. I would say we are stuck here for the night.

VALERIE. (*goes C.*) Who cares what the date is? We're all a lot better off than we were three years ago.

HUGH. Even if you didn't get your Oscar.

VALERIE. Pure jealousy.

EDWINA. (*moves the hassock to the* C. *of the chair beside it and sits*) I tried, didn't I, dear? I kept saying in my column it would be a fitting climax to such a long, long career.

VALERIE. It hasn't been that long.

BETSY. (*crosses back and sits on* R. *end of sofa*) Why, Valerie, I used to see you on the screen when I was still in school.

VALERIE. Then you were retarded. (*moves to bar*)

KITTY. (*enters* D.R. *with demi-tasse poured in cups on tray*) Will everyone take coffee?

VALERIE. Of course. We're normal.

JANE. Ha!

HUGH. (*as KITTY goes to EDWINA*) Kitty, it appears Mr. Garelli might not be showing up after all.

KITTY. Don't surprise me.

EDWINA. It doesn't?

KITTY. No, Ma'am. You see, I've never met him.

VALERIE. (*crosses to* C. *of sofa and sits*) You haven't?

KITTY. No, he hired me through the probation office.

JUSTIN. Probation from what?

KITTY. Prison. (*is in front of EDWINA*) Sugar?

EDWINA. No, thank you. You were incarcerated?

KITTY. No. In Burlington. In the prison.

JANE. (*goes* C.) You're too much.

EDWINA. And you're on probation?

KITTY. (*coffee first to VALERIE, then HUGH and BETSY*) They caught me ouside the A&P with my tote bag full. Three steaks, one chocolate layer cake, and one cantaloupe imported from Mexico.

BETSY. You were shop-lifting to feed your family?

KITTY. No, Ma'am. I just liked the thrill of it.

HUGH. And Mr. Garelli hired you by phone from the office?

KITTY. I get good money and I love to cook.

JANE. And eat.

EDWINA. I've never tasted such good Chicken Kiev.

BETSY. And crepes suzette for dessert. One hardly expected that from a Vermont cook.

KITTY. It's a gift from Heaven. (*goes to the shelves and gets the Ouija Board*)

JANE. (*sits at bar*) How true.

KITTY. Mr. Garelli left instructions that I was to give you this game. He thought it might amuse you.

JANE. Is this your good idea? (*KITTY nods.*)

VALERIE. A contract for SALOME would amuse me.

EDWINA. And the audience no doubt.

KITTY. Here we are. (*Puts game on coffee table, JANE goes to above sofa watching.*)

BETSY. What is it?

KITTY. A Ouija Board. (*pronounces it wee-ja; gets the tray from the shelf*)

HUGH. Ouija. (*pronounces it correctly — wee-gee*) It's a Ouija Board. I haven't seen one of these in years. (*opens box*)

KITTY. I'll go do the dishes and eat a little something.

JANE. (*as KITTY exits* D.R.) A little?

EDWINA. Why do you suppose Stanzio wants us to play this?

BETSY. How do you do it?

HUGH. (*takes out board and the mover*) It's stupid really. We have this board with all the letters of the alphabet on it and then we all put our fingers on this thing, ask it a question, concentrate, and it spells out the answer.

VALERIE. You might as well go to a medium.

EDWINA. (*crosses to sofa and sits* C.) They're all fakes. (*They all get the board ready.*)

JANE. They're not well thought of.

BETSY. This could be intriguing.

JUSTIN. (*rises, crosses in and sits on floor by table*) Shall we have a go?

HUGH. (*looks at his watch*) I have to make a call at eight sharp.

EDWINA. (*brightening to gossip*) Oh. To whom?

HUGH. Nothing to intrigue you, Edwina. Mordecai Zander left a message on my service to call him at eight sharp.

EDWINA. If he wants you to star in that Bible epic he's doing, tell me first.

BETSY. You have a few minutes yet, Hugh. Let's play this thing.

VALERIE. You will mention me as co-star if Mordecai wants you, won't you, darling?

JANE. (*by VALERIE's L.*) You're so Biblical.

BETSY. What shall we ask this thing?

EDWINA. How about, "Is Betsy and Hugh's marriage straining at the leash?"

JANE. That's a goody.

HUGH. Edwina!

BETSY. We're as happy as the day we were married, aren't we, darling?

HUGH. Idyllically so. (*They kiss.*)

VALERIE. How sweet.

JANE. (*looking down at them*) How sickening.

JUSTIN. Come on, let's play. (*puts his fingers on the mover*)

VALERIE. It's a stupid fake. That thing's not going to move by itself.

JANE. Yes, it is. (*moves below the table, puts her fingers on it and gives it a sharp thrust*)

JUSTIN. Oh, my God!

EDWINA. You did that.

JUSTIN. No, I didn't. I swear I didn't. It just went by itself.

VALERIE. We'll see about that. Let's all put our fingers on it. Then we'll know. (*JANE kneels on the floor below the coffee table.*)

JUSTIN. You'll see.

BETSY. If it happens again. (*They all put their fingers on it.*)

HUGH. We must look rather stupid sitting here like this.

EDWINA. Nothing's happening. (*JANE puts her finger on top of theirs.*)

BETSY. But it is. It's starting to move. (*JANE makes it go in fast circles.*)

JUSTIN. Now do you believe me?

VALERIE. This is wierd.

EDWINA. Is anyone moving this?

VALERIE. No, it's going by itself.

HUGH. As if someone were pushing it. (*They are all talking in low voices, they feel eerie.*)

BETSY. I'm going to let go.

JUSTIN. No, let's see what happens.

HUGH. But we haven't asked it a question.

EDWINA. It's stopping at letters now. It's asking us something.

JANE. This is fun.

JUSTIN. (*reads letters as the mover stops at them.*) W-h-o k-i-l-l-e-d J-a-n-e?

EDWINA. Who killed Jane?

JANE. (*rises, crosses to windows via* C.) That's the sixty-four dollar question.

BETSY. (*Rises, crosses to window, she is beside JANE.*) I don't like this. It's ridiculous.

EDWINA. This whole evening is ridiculous.

JUSTIN. (*rises and crosses below chair*) But why are we here, that's what I want to know.

BETSY. (*turns and looks directly towards JANE*) Who arranged this weekend if Stanzio didn't? I feel we're being manipulated by someone.

JANE. (*in BETSY's face*) You're getting warmer.

BETSY. But who? And why?

VALERIE. (*goes to bar*) I'm going to manipulate some brandy into this coffee.

JUSTIN. And I'm going to follow the leader. (*goes to bar via* L. *of chair*)

HUGH. I'd better make that phone call. When Mordecai says eight he means eight sharp. (*exits into library closing door*)

BETSY. (*moves above sofa*) No one answered my question. Why are we all here and why on the anniversary of Jane's death?

JUSTIN. And who's conscience ruled the Ouija board?

JANE. (*as she runs off* D.R.) Kitty, the game worked. They're all upset.

EDWINA. (*looking towards library*) I'd love to know if Hugh is going to star for Mordecai. (*rises and goes to library*) I'll just tip-toe in there for something. A Kleenex.

BETSY. Why would there be a Kleenex in the library?

EDWINA. Well, I'll think of some excuse. (*goes into library closing door*)

VALERIE. (*sits at the bar*) What I wouldn't give to get some dirt on her.

JUSTIN. We all know she trades a good mention in the column for a hot item.

VALERIE. Like you getting drunk in the Tijuana plaza and doing the Mexican Hat Dance naked as a jay bird?

Edwina gave me a whole paragraph for that one. (*smiles at him knowingly*)

JUSTIN. And who do you think told her about you and that ski instructor in St. Moritz? (*returns the same smile*)

EDWINA. (*comes out of library with Kleenex*) I got the Kleenex. (*closes door*)

BETSY. (*moves* C.) But what's Hugh saying?

EDWINA. (*goes to BETSY*) He hasn't gotten Mordecai yet. There was no answer.

BETSY. (*goes below EDWINA to the library*) I bet Mordecai's at Eileen's. I'll give him her number. (*exits library, closes door*)

EDWINA. Eileen Enders? I didn't know about that.

VALERIE. (*happily*) I did. We all did, didn't we, Justin?

JUSTIN. (*goes to library door and tries to listen*) I suppose it's time he got around to Eileen. Everyone else in Southern California has.

EDWINA. Why didn't you tell me?

VALERIE. (*with a smile*) And betray a confidence? Darling, what do you take me for?

EDWINA. Do you want a direct answer?

VALERIE. No. (*goes below her to sofa*) Have a drink instead.

EDWINA. I never touch alcohol.

VALERIE. It's all right, dear, you're among enemies. (*sits on sofa as EDWINA pours a straight scotch*)

JUSTIN. Take it easy, Valerie.

VALERIE. She can't do me any harm. We're all in this together. We've got to trust each other, don't we, Edwina?

EDWINA. We expose one of us, we expose all of us. (*drinks it down straight*)

VALERIE. Taking it straight?

EDWINA. (*glares at her*) I was just bitten by a snake.

BETSY. (*Comes out of library almost hitting JUSTIN; she closes the door.*) Hugh's calling Eileen's. (*JUSTIN sits in chair.*) Strange Mordecai wasn't home. He said eight sharp.

VALERIE. Did you remind Hugh to say I'd be perfect casting?

BETSY. (*smiles, crosses* C.) Oh, darling, I forgot. What a silly I am.

VALERIE. (*starts for library*) I'll do it myself.

BETSY. But the part's so young. They'd have to put more than gauze over the camera. Maybe plaster of Paris?

VALERIE. At least I wear costumes well. In your first film, I understand you didn't wear any. (*exits, closing door*)

EDWINA. (*goes* C.) Is that true, Betsy?

BETSY. (*sits* R. *on sofa*) I'll never tell you, Edwina.

JUSTIN. Since we're all stuck here together, can't we at least be more friendly?

EDWINA. (*goes to sofa*) You're not good enough actors.

BETSY. At least we have a decent career. Look at you. All you do is live vicariously through us.

JUSTIN. (*as the fighting has increased*) Will you both shut up! (*They do.*)

JANE. (*enters* D.R. *followed by KITTY who is finishing a banana*) You should have seen them with the Ouija Board.

KITTY. I thought you'd like that. (*looks at them*) What's the matter with everyone?

JANE. I sense the slings and arrows of outrageous friends.

VALERIE. (*enters, closes door*) Hugh must be getting

an earfull. He's just sitting there in that big leather chair looking out the window and listening.

JUSTIN. And you didn't mention me as director?

VALERIE. I ran out of ink. (*goes to bar*)

JUSTIN. (*rises*) No one can direct those Biblical epics better than me and Cecil B. DeMille and he's dead. (*goes into library closing door*)

EDWINA. I wish there was an extension in here. Wouldn't you love to know what he's saying?

BETSY. He'll tell me later but you'll never know. (*to VALERIE*) I gather he's got Mordecai?

VALERIE. How do I know? He was listening to someone. I just slipped my note to the front of the desk.

BETSY. I didn't know you could write.

VALERIE. (*sits at bar*) It said, "Remind him of me." Not one word over two syllables.

JUSTIN. (*enters closing door*) It must be important. He's listening and not saying a word.

EDWINA. (*rises and goes to library*) If he gets the lead it will be his first costume picture since IVANHOE. (*listens at door.*)

VALERIE. (*joins her listening*) Edwina, that's eavesdropping.

JANE. Isn't that a sin?

KITTY. Not one of the ten deadly.

BETSY. (*crosses to them*) You have no right to listen.

EDWINA. (*We can hear mumblings but not distinct words.*) He's talking now.

VALERIE. What's he saying?

JUSTIN. You women are horrible. (*Joins them; they are all crowded at the door.*) What *is* he saying?

EDWINA. I can't hear the words really. Just the —(*Sound of gunshot from library. They jump back. JANE and KITTY cross* C.)

JUSTIN. (*as they all speak at once*) What was that?

EDWINA. Oh, my God!

BETSY. Hugh!

KITTY. I hadn't planned on this.

VALERIE. (*as JUSTIN goes into library leaving door open*) Be careful, Justin.

BETSY. (*as she starts into library and EDWINA holds her back*) Let me go!

EDWINA. Not yet. Wait.

JANE. What can we do?

KITTY. I'm out of my depth.

JUSTIN. (*comes out of library*) Hugh's dead. Shot.

BETSY. No!

VALERIE. But how? Who?

JANE. The gun is there. We are here. It has to be suicide.

KITTY. (*goes* D.C.) Hold it right there! (*gestures and they all freeze except JANE*)

JANE. (*crosses to her*) Hugh didn't shoot himself any more than I pushed myself downstairs.

KITTY. (*gets book from shelves*) I think you're right.

JANE. Kitty, what will we do?

KITTY. (*brings book back to JANE at* C.) I don't think there's anything about this in the book. The rules are broken.

JANE. You know what this means? Our wings are clipped before we ever get them. (*They look at each other as the curtain falls.*)

ACT TWO

It is several hours later. JANE and KITTY are standing
D.C. with JANE on the R. The others are in a freeze,
VALERIE is at the bar about to pour a drink, BETSY
is sitting in the chair, JUSTIN on the sofa, ED-
WINA is in the library.

KITTY. (*to audience*) Are you over the shock? I bet you were as surprised as we were.

JANE. (*front*) Why don't I even feel sad? Hugh is dead.

KITTY. We know it's nothing to be sad about.

JANE. Shouldn't I be crying? I'm a widow.

KITTY. Hugh married again.

JANE. Then I'm a widow once removed.

KITTY. Betsy is the one who should be crying.

JANE. (*goes to BETSY R. of sofa*) She's too busy plotting her future. Look at them. No one looks depressed or even upset.

KITTY. (*goes to library door*) Edwina's happy as a lark phoning in her scoop.

JANE. Do they really believe Hugh killed himself?

KITTY. (*crosses below chair to sofa looking at them*) Their thoughts are more on themselves than on Hugh.

JANE. You're sure you can't take us back to watch the shooting?

KITTY. It's not possible.

JANE. Look in your book.

KITTY. (*goes to the book on shelves*) I already did. (*JANE goes to her.*) But they don't make things that simple. See. (*shows her the book*)

JANE. (*reads*) "Violence. Non-returnable." (*to KITTY*) Its like liquor bottles. (*reads*) "You can't go back again".

53

KITTY. That part was written by Thomas Wolfe.

JANE. Then what shall we do?

KITTY. (*takes book*) Start time going again and see what happens.

JANE. (*crosses* C.) It's strange but I don't seem to care very much any more.

KITTY. Think of me. I want to go through the gates. Just wait until you're this close.

JANE. (*sits on hassock*) Why should I have to wait? I led an exemplary life.

KITTY. (*crosses* C.) They count every little misdemeanor up there. (*pulls JANE's form out of the book*) Let's see. Here you are. Shall I start back in high school when you cheated on Algebra Two?

JANE. I don't even remember Algebra One.

KITTY. —right through that illicit weekend in Palm Springs with—

JANE. All right, all right, I believe you.

KITTY. (*goes to shelves and puts book down*) After you've helped a few sinners repent, you'll get a big case and then the gates will open.

JANE. It's like standing in line for the second show at Radio City Music Hall.

KITTY. (*goes* D.C., *to audience*) Let's pick up a few hours later. The local authorities have come and gone and the—what shall I call Hugh?

JANE. Corpus delicti?

KITTY. (*smiles*) I love it. The corpus—whatever-it-is —is gone. Ready. On the count of three. (*goes* D.R.) One—two—three. (*Makes a gesture and they all become animated. VALERIE continues pouring her drink. We can hear EDWINA on the phone in the library.*)

VALERIE. Do you think that State Trooper is a direct descendant of Johnny Appleseed?

JUSTIN. He's just temporary. The city boys will be here in the morning when the roads are passable.

VALERIE. (*goes* C.) I hope we get a Dirty Harry.

BETSY. I don't see why anyone has to come. Hugh is dead. It's obvious he shot himself.

VALERIE. Maybe Mordecai didn't give him the part. (*goes towards JUSTIN*) Knowing Hugh, that would surely unhinge him.

JANE. It's just like that overdose of sleeping pills you took when PASSION IN PAGO-PAGO made all the ten worst lists of the year.

BETSY. Publicity, Justin. She didn't take enough to kill her, did you, Valerie? Besides, she phoned her agent and the Los Angeles Herald before she collapsed.

VALERIE. I'd lost count of the pills. (*crosses to windows*)

BETSY. I know a dozen people who would gladly have helped you count.

JANE. I'd have gotten you a refill.

JUSTIN. I'm delighted to see how upset you both are. Hugh is barely at the Pearly Gates.

KITTY. (*sits sofa* R.) Whoever started that rumor about pearl?

BETSY. I'm still in shock. I'll cry tomorrow.

VALERIE. That's a good title.

JANE. She'll cry in front of the TV cameras.

VALERIE. (*goes* C.) I suppose you'll be in a sweet little black suit by Yves St. Laurent?

BETSY. (*rises*) Perry Ellis. American, darling, stay American. It's good for the image. (*goes to bar and pours a drink*)

JANE. What one has to think of in time of grief.

JUSTIN. Edwina is probably wrecking your image right now to both the AP and UP.

VALERIE. I hope she says how distraught I am.

JUSTIN. She's been on the phone long enough to dictate a book.

VALERIE. (*goes to library*) Let's open the door just a tiny bit.

JUSTIN. You might not like it.

BETSY. (*as she joins VALERIE*) It's for our own good.

JANE. (*crosses above sofa to KITTY*) Isn't it marvelous how they rationalize?

VALERIE. Maybe Edwina can get them to use a picture of me.

BETSY. I'm the grieving widow. (*opens door and we hear EDWINA audibly*)

EDWINA. (*offstage*) . . . slumped in the chair looking out the window at the mountains, looking at his future . . .

KITTY. That's good writing?

JANE. (*perches on back of sofa by KITTY*) She can make a whole sentence if she works at it.

EDWINA. (*offstage*) The revolver lay on the floor by his side, smoke curling from the barrel.

JUSTIN. (*rises and goes below chair*) I didn't see any smoke.

VALERIE. Poetic license.

EDWINA. (*offstage*) . . . as the life force left one of our greatest actors. His bereaved and shocked widow—

BETSY. Make it good.

EDWINA. (*offstage*)—well-known actress Betsy Randolph collapsed and had to be sedated.

JANE. She had a straight Scotch.

EDWINA. (*offstage*) Valerie Vickers, a dear friend of the Lawton's, immediately contacted her guru and is in meditation. Justin Wills, the famed director, took command and directed the local authorities.

JANE. He just sat there with his mouth open like a guppie.

JUSTIN. I will be a pall bearer, won't I, Betsy?

BETSY. (*smiles at him*) I will be in your next picture, won't I, Justin?

KITTY. And I thought people were discovered at Schwab's Drug Store.

EDWINA. (*offstage*) Your reporter, an intimate of the deceased, put her tears on the back burner—

JANE. Block that metaphor.

EDWINA. (*offstage*)—to break the news to the world that Hugh Lawton had acted his last scene, a death scene with no audience. The grim reaper has called "Cut" to a brilliant career.

VALERIE. That won't keep the Pulitzer prize committee awake.

EDWINA. (*offstage*) I'll call you later with the funeral arrangements.

VALERIE. (*to BETSY*) Forest Lawn?

JANE. Naturally.

BETSY. (*agreeing*) Forest Lawn.

EDWINA. (*offstage*) And don't run a smiling picture of me. Something wistful. Use that one from the DYNASTY party. That had a sad, far-away look.

VALERIE. That was no far-away look. That was three martinis.

EDWINA. (*offstage*) I'll get back to you. (*She hangs up the phone, JUSTIN rushes to the sofa and sits, VALERIE hurries to the bar stool, and BETSY to the hassock.*)

KITTY. Whatever happened to the mourning period?

JANE. That's reserved for the press. This will raise

Betsy's salary by a good ten per cent.

EDWINA. (*comes to the library door*) Did you like my story?

VALERIE. (*all innocence*) What story?

BETSY. Were you calling the papers?

EDWINA. I could see your reflection in the window. You were huddled together like the Gish Sisters in ORPHANS OF THE STORM.

BETSY. I depend on you, Edwina. You must sit beside me at the funeral.

EDWINA. (*sits in chair*) I'll be right there, dear.

JUSTIN. (*rises and goes C.*) I'll direct it for you, Betsy. We'll use Gombo from Hugh's African triumph.

JANE. (*to KITTY*) Gombo's an elephant.

JUSTIN. Draped in black, his trunk hanging down dejectedly waving Hugh's portrait back and forth.

KITTY. This is a funeral?

JANE. This is Hollywood.

BETSY. I'll walk beside the elephant.

VALERIE. How will we know which is Gombo?

BETSY. I'll be deeply veiled.

EDWINA. Not too deeply. Be sure the public sees your face.

BETSY. And I'll have a small get-together in the Grand Ballroom of the Beverly Wilshire.

JANE. Life must go on.

VALERIE. I wonder if there's a tv series in Hugh's life.

EDWINA. Hardly in the one the public knows.

VALERIE. Why not? They've done Flynn, Valentino, Princess Grace.

BETSY. Who could we get young enough to play you, Valerie?

VALERIE. Very funny. (*looks in the ice bucket*) There's no ice.

JUSTIN. Our dear friend is dead and you're worried about ice?

VALERIE. How can I grieve when I'm thirsty? (*crosses* c.) Where the hell is that shop-lifting maid?

KITTY. (*rises and goes* D.R.) I'd better get to the kitchen.

JUSTIN. Weeping in the pantry no doubt.

JANE. (*goes* D.R. *calling after KITTY who exits*) And weep.

KITTY. (*offstage*) Buckets.

VALERIE. (*crosses to archway as JANE goes above sofa*) What's her name again?

BETSY. How do I know?

EDWINA. Try Minerva.

JUSTIN. Or Annie.

VALERIE. (*calls*) Darling!

EDWINA. Stand back. It sounds like you're calling hogs.

KITTY. (*enters in tears*) What? What do you want?

VALERIE. Ice, dear. In this bucket. It's for Miss Randolph's head. This has brought on one of her migraines.

KITTY. (*to BETSY as she goes to her*) How about some nice, hot chicken neck soup?

BETSY. Just ice.

VALERIE. In this bucket.

KITTY. I can't believe it. Mr. Lawton was so happy at dinner laughing and joking and then to go and — and — (*bursts into big tears*)

JANE. (*crosses to KITTY and back above sofa*) You're overacting.

VALERIE. You just get some ice. Life must go on, dear.

KITTY. I know. (*takes bucket*) As Mr. Lawton said in that picture, it's a far, far better rest he goes to now than he has ever known. (*goes off* D.R. *dramatically*)

JANE. Rest? He's filling out forms. (*VALERIE
returns to bar.*)

BETSY. That was Ronald Colman's line, wasn't it?

EDWINA. That's my lead-in for tomorrow's article.

JANE. I've got to get back to L.A. first thing in the
morning. I don't care about the authorities. I'll get the
company lawyers on it. I'm overbudget already.

BETSY. I think I'll hire a jet to take the body back. Do
they take Master Charge?

VALERIE. (*moves to BETSY*) It will land in L.A. and
you'll just manage to get down the stairs before you
faint gracefully to the ground.

JANE. You've got it.

BETSY. With my face to the cameras. Jealous,
Valerie? (*Goes to bar for a drink, VALERIE goes to
windows.*)

EDWINA. You bet she is. And I get to write all that
sentimental drivel on your innermost feelings. That's
part of our deal.

BETSY. Why Hugh shot himself is not connected with
THE LOVES OF LAURA.

VALERIE. Isn't it?

EDWINA. (*rises and goes* C.) Think about it, dear.
We're invited up here for the weekend by Stanzio
Garelli, but he's gone to London. It's the third anniversary of Jane's death, that Ouija thing goes bonkers and
then Hugh dies. That's stretching coincidence into the
twilight zone.

JUSTIN. If we all wondered about Jane's death, how
do we feel about Hugh's?

BETSY. (*crosses to library door*) He was alone in the
library, we heard him on the phone, the shot rang out.
Obviously it was suicide.

VALERIE. Was it?

JANE. No.

JUSTIN. Yes. Unless —

EDWINA. What?

JUSTIN. Unless someone in this room is very clever.

VALERIE. We're all very clever, darling. That's our business.

BETSY. (*steps in*) Justin, you're not trying to say that one of us is a murderer?

JANE. Isn't he?

JUSTIN. Aren't I?

KITTY. (*Comes in with filled ice bucket and puts it on bar; she sniffles.*) Ice! (*BETSY goes below bar and sits on stool.*)

VALERIE. Thank you, dear. You're a good girl.

JANE. (*by VALERIE*) I'm surprised you recognize one.

KITTY. (*to BETSY*) I've made you a nice hot cup of cocoa with a marshmallow floating on top.

BETSY. I couldn't, thank you.

KITTY. Then I'll have to drink it myself.

VALERIE. (*crosses to KITTY at c.*) You can go home now. Do your chores, milk the cows.

KITTY. No, Ma'am. I sleep over.

JANE. (*above sofa*) So does Valerie — usually.

VALERIE. (*her arm on KITTY, she takes her D.R.*) You go to bed then. I know how upset you are. I could give you Seconal.

KITTY. No, Ma'am, I don't read books. (*VALERIE gives us, crosses back to bar for drink.*)

JANE. No one is that stupid.

KITTY. I'll go curl up with the radio and listen to the stock market.

JUSTIN. Let me know how IBM does.

KITTY. I mean the real stock market, beef and lamb and pork bellies. (*exits*)

VALERIE. Pork bellies?

JUSTIN. Would you prefer pork stomachs?

VALERIE. It sounds disgusting.

BETSY. (*rises and crosses to stairs*) I'm not going to sit here all night talking about pigs' anatomy. I have a lot to think about. I am going to bed.

JUSTIN. (*rises and goes to BETSY*) Do the bedroom doors have locks?

EDWINA. We're not in any danger.

JUSTIN. Aren't we? There were five of us on THE LOVES OF LAURA deal. That Swiss bank account is now quartered. If one more goes then it will be divided into thirds. Yes, I'm going to lock my door.

BETSY. I think we all are. (*Phone rings in the library.*)

JUSTIN. I'll get it before that bucolic wonder gallops in here again. (*exits library and closes door*)

VALERIE. She's too involved with pork toes.

JANE. If it's for me it's long distance. (*JUSTIN's voice can be heard from library.*)

VALERIE. (*goes to library door*) Justin's really serious about the possibility of murder, isn't he?

EDWINA. I agree we'd gladly slit each other's throats figuratively but I don't think we'd stoop to murder.

VALERIE. Edwina, that's the nicest thing you've ever said.

BETSY. (*goes* D.C.) All that money collecting in Switzerland. Which of us could use it most? Justin is banking his whole career on this new movie—

EDWINA. And from what I hear it's another HEAVEN'S GATE.

JANE. (*goes above sofa*) They don't like that title up there.

BETSY. Valerie, your career is slowing down unless you want to play mothers.

VALERIE. And you can't go on playing sweet things much longer. You can only fool the public for so long.

EDWINA. Yes, Betsy, if your tv series bombs, you'll be like one of the cast-offs from CHARLEY'S ANGELS.

JANE. (*goes above sofa to its* R.) They don't like that title either.

VALERIE. (*goes to bar*) And Edwina, now that the public is forgiving us for our sins, your exposé days are numbered.

BETSY. (*crosses below JANE and goes to sofa* R.) So we all have a reason not to mourn Hugh too much.

JUSTIN. (*comes back from library*) The mystery deepens.

EDWINA. Who was it?

JUSTIN. Mordecai just heard the news on the radio. He was calling to see if he could do anything.

BETSY. His private jet. Perfect.

JUSTIN. (*goes* C.) I asked him how Hugh sounded when he called and guess what?

EDWINA. He didn't get Mordecai?

JUSTIN. Not only that but Mordecai never even left a message for Hugh to call at eight o'clock.

JANE. (*goes* D.R.) That does it!

EDWINA. It was murder!

VALERIE. (*crosses to above hassock*) It couldn't be. We were all in here.

JUSTIN. If one of us did dispatch Hugh to the great cutting room in the sky—

JANE. You'll never be an author.

JUSTIN. —then I think she—

VALERIE. (*sits on the hassock*) Or he. Don't forget yourself, darling.

JUSTIN. Whoever of us it is better stop right now.

JANE. (*sits* R. *on sofa*) Too late for me.

JUSTIN. We all have a fortune we'll pick up in Switzerland in two years but one of us is getting too greedy.

VALERIE. Isn't that in character for any of us?

JUSTIN. I think we should agree if one more of us meets an untimely end the others should tell the truth of our arrangement.

VALERIE. That sounds like blackmail.

JUSTIN. Let's call it insurance.

EDWINA. (*rises*) I think Justin's quite right. Whoever it is had better stop right now.

VALERIE. Agreed.

BETSY. Agreed.

JUSTIN. (*goes to* R. *of stairs*) Now let's all go upstairs and lock our doors.

EDWINA. (*goes upstairs*) What an article this would make for a Sunday magazine.

VALERIE. Unless you're too dead to write it.

BETSY. Maybe it's her. Is it you, Edwina?

EDWINA. (*on landing followed by BETSY and VALERIE*) You all know I don't have the intelligence for that sort of thing. For once I'm glad I'm just a silly, nonsensical little woman. (*exits*)

BETSY. I wonder.

JANE. So do I.

BETSY. Well, it isn't me. One doesn't kill one's own family. (*exits*)

VALERIE. Try telling that to Lizzie Borden.

JUSTIN. Go on, Valerie, let's get upstairs.

VALERIE. (*turns to him on stairs*) Afraid to be left alone with me?

JUSTIN. Of course not.

VALERIE. (*advances on him steadily with an ominous tone to her voice*) You should be. I might kill you right now.

JUSTIN. (*backs up a step*) Valerie!

VALERIE. (*breaks the mood and pats his cheek*) You see, Justin, I can put fear into audiences. (*goes upstairs followed by JUSTIN*) Now, darling, if you ever decide to remake REBECCA, I'll play Mrs. Danvers. I'd gladly cover my natural beauty.

JUSTIN. You mean you'd take off your street make-up?

VALERIE. You really think you have a sense of humor, don't you? (*They are off.*)

JANE. If they're my dearest friends, who are my enemies? Now what? (*rises and comes down to audience*) What would you do if you were me? One thing I know. Hugh didn't shoot himself. He has a good career, a new movie he's starring in, and he's married to Little Miss Fauntleroy. On second thought, maybe he did shoot himself. No, he's too conceited. He'd kill himself in the Hollywood Bowl. I know. I'll return to the scene of the crime and look for clues. I'll find out who killed him. (*Starts for library as HUGH comes charging out; he now wears same grey make-up as she does.*)

HUGH. I hope the hell you do!

JANE. Hugh! (*gives a small scream, backs up and sits arm of the chair*)

HUGH. Aren't you glad to see me?

JANE. Ghosts frighten me.

HUGH. I didn't mean to become one so soon.

JANE. (*Angry, she rises.*) You come bursting out of there without any warning. Why didn't you gently descend with some harp music?

HUGH. (*crosses* C.) It's all been so quick. I'm all confused. We're not really prepared for this dying business.

JANE. You'll like it once you get used to it.

HUGH. I must say you're looking very well. Dying agrees with you.

JANE. Sweet talk will get you nowhere.

HUGH. I see you're in one of your moods.

JANE. I can rise above them now. I can rise above almost anything except your marriage to Betsy.

HUGH. Let's not get trivial. Let's have a drink. (*goes to bar*)

JANE. (*crosses to bar*) You won't like it any more.

HUGH. (*picks up bottle*) Nonsense. (*smells it*) Ohh, you're right.

JANE. I usually am. Will you answer a direct question with a direct answer? Did you commit suicide?

HUGH. No. Is that direct enough.

JANE. I knew it.

HUGH. (*smiles and moves closer to her*) Did you think I shot myself to be with you?

JANE. (*crosses away to sofa*) Don't pull that smile on me. It might charm the public but all I see is capped teeth.

HUGH. (*crosses in* C.) Are we going to spend eternity bickering?

JANE. You have a lot to learn.

HUGH. Are we still — I mean, are you still my — what is our status? Is my marriage to Betsy annulled?

JANE. I believe you once said to me, "Till death us do part". Well, we're dead and we're parted. (*goes below him to chair*)

HUGH. I can fly by and see you sometimes, can't I?

JANE. You don't have any wings and I don't see you sprouting any in the immediate future.

HUGH. Since I'm no angel, let's get out of here. Let's go back to —

JANE. That little place outside Manzanillo?

HUGH. (*smiles*) You remember?

JANE. (*sits in chair*) I remember, Betsy remembers, and the female half of the Screen Actor's Guild remembers.

HUGH. You're bitter.

JANE. You're damned right I'm bitter.

HUGH. (*sits on hassock*) This isn't much fun. I sort of thought one just floated around enjoying oneself.

JANE. You have to pay for your sins, Hugh, darling, and they don't take American Express.

HUGH. All my sins? How depressing.

JANE. First you fill out forms.

HUGH. Yes, I'd just gotten up there and was handed a pile of papers when I was rushed back down here again.

JANE. That's because I was thinking of you.

HUGH. (*smiles and leans towards her*) Were you, darling?

JANE. (*rises and goes* D.C.) I am trying to find out who murdered me and —

HUGH. You fell downstairs and hit your head.

JANE. (*turns to him*) I will say this once more and then it will never cross my lips again. I was pushed.

HUGH. Really?

JANE. I suppose you don't remember who shot you?

HUGH. (*rises and goes to library*) I was trying to get through to Mordecai. I was sitting in that big leather chair of Stanzio's looking out at the snow and then there was a sharp noise.

JANE. The gun shot.

HUGH. But it turned into beautiful music. It was like Guy Lombardo playing AULD LANG SYNE.

JANE. And you were in the waiting room?

HUGH. (*goes to her*) Sitting next to this perfectly adorable ingenue. Her skimobile went off a cliff near

Sugarbush while she was wrapped in the arms of her lover. Isn't that romantic?

JANE. (*sits* R. *on sofa*) The point is you were murdered, I was murdered, and I want to find out who did it so I can start knocking some demerits off my score.

HUGH. And then what?

JANE. Then I can go through the gates.

HUGH. The pearly ones?

JANE. That's just publicity. They are not pearl.

HUGH. (*sits by her*) Will you save me a nice cloud with a giant tv screen and casettes of my old movies?

JANE. By the time you pay for your sins television will be obsolete.

HUGH. Do they know everything?

JANE. They have total recall and just what I know about you would make a mini-series. In three parts.

HUGH. You know very little about me.

JANE. I'm learning. (*rises and crosses* C.) You weren't exactly Old Faithful.

HUGH. You can't count the sins of the flesh now that I don't have any flesh.

JANE. Don't try to wheedle out of it.

HUGH. (*Rises; they are both working up to a fight.*) You're being petty again.

JANE. Petty is so far down on the list of sins it's like cheating at solitaire.

HUGH. (*goes to her*) Still one with the flip line, aren't you?

JANE. And my delivery is better than yours.

HUGH. How dare you criticize my acting.

JANE. You were nothing without make-up, a dialogue coach, and a good editor. You were a product of other people like a giant Barbie Doll. (*KITTY comes in from* D.R. *munching a cookie.*)

HUGH. (*now they are both furious*) And what about you? The great author. It's us actors make you look good.

KITTY. Well, well, well. And I thought marriages were made in Heaven.

HUGH. Who the devil are you?

KITTY. I'm no devil.

JANE. This is Kitty.

HUGH. Are you human or what?

KITTY. I'm a what. I'm helping Jane find out who pushed her.

HUGH. Sort of an astral detective?

JANE. Really, Hugh, you are so boring. Kitty is from up there and once she helps me find my murderer she's going through the gates.

HUGH. Has it taken you a long time to get this far?

KITTY. (*sits on sofa*) What's a couple of centuries here or there?

JANE. Hugh will have to think in milleniums.

KITTY. Isn't it time you two kissed and made up?

HUGH. Are we allowed to kiss?

KITTY. Of course.

HUGH. (*goes to JANE*) And do we—

JANE. No, Hugh, we don't. (*moves away L.*)

KITTY. Jane, you're not still humanly angry, are you?

JANE. (*sighs*) Somehow I can't seem to stay that way any longer.

KITTY. Now go and kiss Hugh.

HUGH. I can't wait.

JANE. All right, (*goes to him and kisses the air somewhere near his face and drifts away again above the sofa*)

HUGH. That was it? That was a kiss?

JANE. (*smiles and leans over back of sofa*) That's all you get up there.

HUGH. (*sits on hassock*) I don't think I'm ready for Heaven yet.

KITTY. I'm sure Heaven isn't ready for you. (*rises and goes* C.) Now can we get back to the murders?

HUGH. Yes. Who shot me?

JANE. (*goes to sofa* R.) Undoubtedly your present wife.

HUGH. Not Betsy. She adores me.

JANE. Did they all adore you, Edwina, Valerie, and even Justin?

KITTY. (*goes to library*) I think we should look for clues in the library.

HUGH. I don't want to go back in there again.

JANE. (*goes below stairs*) If I can look at the stairs, you can look at the library. (*notices someone coming from upstairs*) Someone's coming.

HUGH. (*rises and goes to bar*) Hide. We have to hide.

JANE. (*goes to him*) You're so naive. No one can see us.

KITTY. Except me if I want them to. You watch in here and I'll case the library. (*exits*)

HUGH. If ghosts like us can walk into movie theatres without paying, it ruins my percentages of the gross. I should call my lawyer.

JANE. It doesn't matter any more, dear.

HUGH. Oh, that's right. (*JUSTIN comes down stairs.*)

JANE. Justin. Now, what does he want?

HUGH. He's covering up something. I knew he was a killer.

JANE. (*As JUSTIN goes to bar and pours a drink he is between them.*) I think he's just going to kill a bottle.

HUGH. He doesn't look like a murderer, does he?

JANE. Neither did Baby Face Nelson.

BETSY. (*from landing*) Justin Wills, whatever are you doing down here?

JANE. Ah, the prom queen.

JUSTIN. Having a repeat nightcap. (*BETSY comes downstairs and crosses to sofa, JUSTIN goes U.C.*)

HUGH. She is lovely.

JANE. So was Medea.

JUSTIN. What are you doing?

BETSY. I heard someone and wondered who it was. (*sits on sofa and leans back seductively*)

JANE. It's going to be one of those seduction scenes.

HUGH. I'm hardly dead yet.

JUSTIN. Drink?

BETSY. No, thank you.

JANE. You carried on when I was alive.

JUSTIN. (*goes to stairs*) Then I'll wander back to bed and leave you to whatever you really came down here to do.

BETSY. I was restless but I shouldn't be alone with you. After all, if I'm not the killer then it's you or Edwina or Valerie.

JUSTIN. (*crosses to sofa*) It isn't me.

BETSY. When I went into the library, Hugh could already have been dead. He was faced away from me.

JUSTIN. (*sits on sofa*) And when I went in, after you I might add, he could already have been dead.

BETSY. Except we all heard him on the phone before he was shot.

JUSTIN. Then it must have been a ghost.

BETSY. I don't believe in ghosts.

HUGH. (*crosses beside JANE*) You should.

JUSTIN. Neither do I. Wouldn't it be embarrassing to have a couple of bits of ectoplasm standing beside us?

BETSY. I imagine we could smell them.

HUGH. That's disgusting.

JANE. (*blows on BETSY*) Take that.

BETSY. Oh, there's a terrible draft. (*rises and goes to stairs*) I'm going to bed. Then you can do whatever you want down here.

JUSTIN. (*rises and goes to stairs*) I've gotten my drink. Shall we go up together and then we won't wonder what the other was really up to?

BETSY. You're so clever.

JUSTIN. (*as they go upstairs*) I'm distressed to see how much you miss your husband.

BETSY. (*turns on landing*) As one door closes, another opens.

JUSTIN. Perhaps I'm behind it.

BETSY. If there's one thing I need it's a good director.

JUSTIN. I know just how to direct you. (*They exit.*)

HUGH. Well, really!

JANE. (*goes to sofa R. enjoying herself immensely*) Getting a bit of your own back, aren't you?

HUGH. (*goes C.*) She's overcome with grief, that's what it is. She doesn't know what she's doing.

JANE. There isn't a moment that one doesn't know what the score is. It's Betsy Randolph 10, visitors 0.

KITTY. (*enters from library*) What were they doing down here?

JANE. That's what we were wondering.

KITTY. Maybe one of them was looking for this. (*Crosses C. and holds out timer light. It is one of those plugs which goes into the wall and a lamp plugs into it so the lamp goes on and off at preset times.*)

JANE. (*moves in C.*) What's that thing?

HUGH. (*looks at it*) It's one of those light timers. You remember, we had one in the living room.

JANE. That thing that puts the lights on and off when you're away?

HUGH. Brilliant.

JANE. I never could understand how it worked.

HUGH. (*to KITTY*) Where was it?

KITTY. Plugged into an outlet by the bookcase.

JANE. So what's that prove, the lights went on and off?

KITTY. Do you know what was plugged into it? A tape recorder.

HUGH. So it could be set to go on and off?

KITTY. I think just "off" was important.

JANE. What are you getting at?

KITTY. Listen to what's on the tape recorder. I'll wind it back and play it. (*exits library*)

HUGH. She'd make a good Miss Marple.

JANE. Can't you stop thinking about acting for one minute? There are more important things, you know.

HUGH. Really? Like what?

KITTY. (*offstage*) Ready?

HUGH. (*goes below chair*) Shoot.

JANE. Someone did that already. (*calls*) Put it on, Kitty. (*sits on hassock*)

KITTY. (*comes out*) Wait till I close the door. (*Closes the door. We can hear audible but muffled talking from the library.*) There.

JANE. Hugh, that's your voice. That's what we heard just before you were shot.

HUGH. It's my voice all right but I can't hear what I'm saying.

KITTY. It's probably recorded from one of your movies on television. The important thing is it is you talking after you're dead.

JANE. But we heard the shot later.

KITTY. It's at the end of the recording. I'd better turn it off before someone hears it. (*exits library*)

HUGH. How does she know there's a shot on there?

JANE. She has divine guidance.

HUGH. Can't she just ask who the killer is?

JANE. Violence, darling. They don't recognize it.

HUGH. Have they forgotten about the Christians and the lions?

JANE. Nero isn't even allowed in the waiting room yet.

KITTY. (*Comes back with silencer. It is a small round piece of metal that fits on the end of a pistol. She crosses* c.) Now we know Hugh could have been shot any time after he went in there.

HUGH. But how?

KITTY. (*holds out silencer*) Do you know what this is?

JANE. (*rises*) That metal tube? It's part of a socket wrench.

HUGH. No, it's a silencer. I had to use one in a film once.

KITTY. That's right. A silencer was attached to the revolver and removed after you were shot.

HUGH. Where did you find it?

KITTY. Behind one of the books.

JANE. (*goes below sofa*) So when we heard the shot, it was just the recording and Hugh was already dead.

HUGH. And no one knows who did it since I was faced away when each of them came in.

KITTY. All someone had to do was shoot you, take off the silencer, put the gun on the floor beside the chair, set the timer for the tape and then be completely surprised when the gun was supposedly shot later on.

HUGH. And the tape was put on so my voice would come on in a few minutes. Clever, very clever.

JANE. (*sits on sofa*) I wish I were still writing. This would make a dandy Movie of the Week.

HUGH. But we don't know which of them killed me.

KITTY. Not yet, but whoever it is has to cover up his tracks tonight.

JANE. What tracks?

KITTY. If I were the murderer, I'd want to get rid of the timer and the tape and especially this silencer.

JANE. Then all we have to do is wait for whoever it is to come down to remove the evidence.

KITTY. I'd better put it back first. (*exits library*)

JANE. And whoever killed you must have killed me.

HUGH. (*crosses in and sits on sofa*) Not necessarily.

JANE. Why do you say that?

HUGH. Darling, this is rather hard to explain but I did it.

JANE. You killed me.

HUGH. It was rotten of me, I know.

JANE. You hit me on the head with that atrocious statue?

HUGH. And gave you a gentle shove down the stairs. I was gentle, wasn't I?

JANE. (*shocked*) Hugh.

HUGH. I'm terribly sorry.

JANE. You ought to be.

HUGH. It all seems so long ago. It's as if I were looking down through the wrong end of the telescope.

JANE. I know and it doesn't seem too important any more, does it?

HUGH. Not really.

JANE. (*rises and goes above sofa*) If I were still alive, I'd be really furious with you. As it is, I'm just horribly disappointed.

HUGH. The me back then just wanted to marry Betsy and have THE LOVES OF LAURA and there didn't seem to be any way to have both with you in the way.

JANE. Suppose LAURA had been a bomb?

HUGH. I read it one night while you were asleep.

JANE. That's wicked of you, really wicked.

HUGH. I had to think of getting the profits eventually so I xeroxed it and sent it off to all five of us.

JANE. (*crosses to* R. *of sofa*) You really are a louse.

KITTY. (*enters and goes* D.C.) The stage is set. Now all we have to do is wait for the murderer to reappear.

JANE. Kitty, my devoted husband has something to say.

HUGH. I know who killed Jane.

KITTY. Who?

HUGH. Me.

KITTY. (*laughs*) Well, I'll be damned.

HUGH. You're not shocked?

KITTY. You people are too much. You pop in and out of marriage like a yo-yo and then instead of divorce you kill each other.

JANE. I've forgiven him.

HUGH. Isn't that generous of her?

KITTY. Just shows she's getting more celestial.

HUGH. (*to JANE*) Now we'll be together forever.

KITTY. You won't be together. You won't even be in the same waiting room.

HUGH. Why not?

JANE. (*sits sofa* R.) Hugh, you killed me. You'll have to do a lot of good works to make amends, something really important like stopping a war or finding a cure for baldness.

HUGH. That waiting room is so depressing.

KITTY. (*sits sofa* L.) It isn't nearly as nice as ours.

JANE. No suede sofas. You have bleachers.

KITTY. And the walls — apartment house green.

JANE. With grafitti. It makes the subway read like Mother Goose.

KITTY. And the commissary is sickening.

JANE. Instant coffee—

KITTY. McDonald's caters.

JANE. And the desserts—

KITTY. Your choice of Jello or Twinkies.

HUGH. It sounds like hell.

JANE and KITTY. It is!

HUGH. I wish I'd been a better man.

KITTY. They all say that.

JANE. (*sees EDWINA sneaking downstairs*) Look.

HUGH. Edwina.

KITTY. (*crosses to her*) She killed Hugh. (*EDWINA crosses to D.R. arch and looks out, JANE rises and goes above her, HUGH rises and crosses behind her.*)

HUGH. If she goes into the library we've got her.

JANE. (*as EDWINA goes towards library below HUGH*) There she goes.

HUGH. (*JANE and HUGH follow her as KITTY comes down.*) She's after the tape and the silencer. (*EDWINA pauses for a moment to look around and then goes into the library.*) That's it. She shot me.

JANE. (*as they all peer into library*) No, she's going through the desk drawers.

KITTY. Stanzio's papers.

JANE. The snoop.

KITTY. She's found something.

HUGH. She's smirking like the Chesire cat.

EDWINA. (*Comes out holding piece of paper; JANE goes above hassock.*) Stanzio's secret casting list.

JANE. For the new picture.

EDWINA. (*Sits in chair and reads, JANE sits on hassock, KITTY goes above chair and HUGH to the L. of it.*) "Tell Mordecai Eileen Enders can have the lead."

JANE. The springs in his casting couch must be shattered.

EDWINA. "Hugh Lawton—"

HUGH. Yes.

EDWINA. "Overacts"

HUGH. I never overact.

JANE. The truth will out.

EDWINA. "Valerie Vickers. Too old." (*starts for stairs*)

JANE. I love it. I love it. I love it.

HUGH. I'm glad I'm dead.

KITTY. She hasn't got the tape or the silencer.

EDWINA. (*starts upstairs but sees someone coming*) Oh, no!

JANE. Now who's coming?

KITTY. The murderer.

HUGH. (*as EDWINA looks for a place to hide and decides on closet, HUGH has gone to her at* R. *of stairs.*) This is getting like a French farce.

KITTY. Who is it? (*EDWINA goes into the closet.*)

HUGH. (*looks upstairs*) Justin.

JANE. (*goes to* L. *of stairs*) I haven't trusted him since his cowboy version of HAMLET.

JUSTIN. (*rather drunk, crosses* D.R.) I swear I'll join AA.

JANE. (*by the library*) Come on, go into the library.

JUSTIN. Tomorrow. Yes, I'll worry about AA tomorrow. Coffee. I need coffee. (*goes off* D.R.)

JANE. Maybe he'll go into the library after he gets his coffee.

KITTY. Now look here. (*VALERIE comes downstairs carrying an 8 × 10 photo of herself. She crosses to the shelves.*)

JANE. Ah, the ageing leading lady, quite often the murderer.

KITTY. (*They all go to VALERIE.*) What's she up to?

HUGH. (*as VALERIE puts her photo on top of one which is already in a frame*) What is she doing with that photograph?

JANE. Putting her photo over the other one.

KITTY. (*looks closely at photo*) Is that her picture?

JANE. (*goes away* C.) It's so retouched it could be Shirley Temple.

VALERIE. (*looks at photo and smiles*) There, darling, do your best. (*EDWINA pokes her head out of closet.*)

EDWINA. Valerie!

VALERIE. (*turns with a small scream*) Edwina. (*comes* DS. *with photo*) You're going to surprise someone once too often and —

EDWINA. And I'll get murdered? (*JANE sits on the hassock, HUGH crosses to* R. *of EDWINA, KITTY goes by JANE.*) You'd like that, wouldn't you? Then your share of THE LOVES OF LAURA would be even bigger.

VALERIE. I don't need money as much as you, darling. We all know gossip columnists are getting as extinct as the dodo bird.

KITTY. We have dodos up there.

EDWINA. (*takes photo and goes* C.) And what have we here, your graduation picture?

VALERIE. That was taken last month.

EDWINA. Who retouched it, Rembrandt?

VALERIE. (*takes photo and replaces it on shelves as EDWINA sits on the sofa*) It will be worth it tomorrow.

EDWINA. When this place is swarming with the press?

VALERIE. They'll wonder why my photograph is in Stanzio's living room. Oh, won't that cause talk.

EDWINA. I have to admire you, Valerie.

VALERIE. And I admire you, too, Edwina. We're both opportunists.

BETSY. (*offstage upstairs, whispers*) Hello, . . . hello . . .

EDWINA. (*rises*) Who's that?

VALERIE. Betsy.

KITTY. Again?

BETSY. (*offstage*) Who's down there?

VALERIE. What does she want?

JANE. We'd all like to know.

EDWINA. (*goes to closet, HUGH lets her pass*) Let's find out. Will you join me in the closet?

VALERIE. (*goes into closet with her*) I've hidden in them before.

EDWINA. (*as she closes the door*) So I've heard.

JANE. And now the perfect wife suspiciously reappears.

HUGH. (*moves above sofa*) Betsy's no better and no worse than anyone else in the business.

JANE. Depends on what business you think she's in. (*BETSY comes downstairs.*)

BETSY. Who's here?

KITTY. (*goes up to BETSY*) The Three Musketeers and the Bobsey Twins are in the closet.

BETSY. At last I'm alone. (*crosses to library and goes in*)

JANE. (*rises*) She's the killer. I knew it.

HUGH. (*goes below sofa to behind JANE as KITTY goes down to library*) Not Betsy. She loves me desperately.

JANE. (*as she goes to the library*) Desperately might just do it.

HUGH. (*as he and JANE look into library with KITTY trying to see behind them*) Look, she's taking off the tape.

KITTY. (*trying to see through them*) Let me see.

JANE. Now she's going for the timer.

KITTY. Where's the tape?

HUGH. She put it on top of that box of chocolates.

KITTY. What chocolates?

HUGH. The ones on the desk.

KITTY. How did I miss them?

JANE. She's unplugging the timer.

KITTY. (*still trying to see past them*) What kind of chocolates are they?

HUGH. Whitman's Sampler.

KITTY. My favorite.

JANE. She's getting the silencer from behind that book.

KITTY. What book?

JANE. (*turns back to her*) THE BIG SLEEP.

HUGH. How appropriate.

JANE. We've found the murderer. Now you can go through the gates. (*She embraces KITTY.*)

HUGH. She's picking up the tape.

KITTY. Bring the chocolates. Please bring the chocolates.

JANE. (*to HUGH*) She's going to get away with your murder. That's not cricket.

HUGH. (*goes above chair*) Can't we scare her into confessing?

JANE. How?

HUGH. Can't we — what is it — materialize?

JANE. Kitty, can we do that?

KITTY. (*crosses to bar*) It's very difficult.

HUGH. Let's try.

KITTY. (*to their L.*)We have to think very hard. Sit down here. (*HUGH sits on bar stool R. and JANE on L. stool.*) Now close your eyes and concentrate. (*They close their eyes.*)

HUGH. (*after a pause*) Nothing's happening.

JANE. Are you concentrating?

KITTY. All I can think of is those chocolates. Were they gooey ones?

HUGH. The regular assortment. Concentrate.

JANE. I'm starting to feel funny, all tingly.

HUGH. Same here.

KITTY. If it works, act like ghosts.

JANE. How do they act?

HUGH. People think they wave their arms and groan.

JANE. Sounds rather silly.

KITTY. We're materializing. It's working. I know it's working. (*They open their eyes.*)

JANE. I do feel ghostly.

HUGH. Here she comes.

BETSY. (*Comes out of library with tape, silencer, and timer; she goes c. examining them.*) That's done. (*HUGH comes to her R., KITTY to her L., and JANE above her.*)

KITTY. She didn't bring the chocolates.

JANE. Are we ready?

KITTY. On the count of three. One—two—three! (*They all groan, BETSY turns and sees them.*)

BETSY. (*with low horror backs up to sofa*) No—no—Hugh.

HUGH. (*sounding as ghostly as he can*) Yes, it's me.

BETSY. Jane.

JANE. The first wife returns.

BETSY. (*to KITTY*) And who the hell are you?

KITTY. The ghost of Christmas past.

HUGH. You killed me, Betsy.

BETSY. I had to. No, no, stay away from me. (*They close in on her, raise their arms and groan. BETSY screams and faints on sofa.*)

HUGH. We did it. It worked.

KITTY. Now I can get those chocolates. (*exits library*)

VALERIE. (*as she and EDWINA come out of closet*) Who screamed?

EDWINA. Someone else is dead.

VALERIE. (*goes below sofa to BETSY*) It's Betsy.

EDWINA. (*Goes above sofa; JANE and HUGH fade us. watching.*) Is she alive?

JANE. Did we scare her to death?

JUSTIN. (*enters from D.R.*) Someone screamed? What happened?

EDWINA. It's Betsy.

JUSTIN. She's dead.

VALERIE. (*has sat by BETSY*) No, she's fainted.

EDWINA. What's all this. (*picks up the casette and timer*)

JUSTIN. (*goes to EDWINA*) It's a casette tape and —

EDWINA. A light timer.

JANE. Get the silencer.

EDWINA. (*picks up silencer from floor*) And what's this?

JUSTIN. It looks like —

HUGH. A silencer, you idiot.

JUSTIN. Like a silencer for a gun.

VALERIE. What's she doing with those things?

EDWINA. I think I know. (*BETSY stirs.*)

JUSTIN. She's coming round.

KITTY. (*enters library eating chocolate*) There were only two left.

VALERIE. Betsy, darling, what happened?

KITTY. (*delight with her chocolate*) Coconut cream.

BETSY. No, no, I saw — I saw them —

EDWINA. Who?

BETSY. Hugh — Hugh was here and Jane and — some other horrible apparition.

KITTY. Well!

JANE. (*to KITTY as she sits on hassock*) You're not horrible at all.

BETSY. (*almost hysterical*) They know, they've come back for me. They know.

JUSTIN. Know what?

BETSY. That I killed Hugh.

JUSTIN. You didn't!

JANE. She just said she did.

EDWINA. Darling, this is terrible.

JUSTIN. If the authorities find out—

VALERIE. The newspapers—

JUSTIN. No one must know about the Swiss bank account.

EDWINA. All our savings.

VALERIE. Betsy, we're your friends. We'll stick by you.

JUSTIN. What if she tries to kill the rest of us?

BETSY. I wouldn't.

EDWINA. Our lawyers, safe deposit boxes, we'll leave sworn statements against you.

BETSY. I won't kill. Never again.

EDWINA. (*helps her stand*) Come along, dear. We'll take you upstairs and get you a cold cloth.

VALERIE. (*She and JUSTIN help BETSY to the stairs, EDWINA carries the props.*) And we'll rehearse what we'll say to the police.

JUSTIN. I'll direct it.

VALERIE. And I'll give Edwina an acting lesson. (*They are going upstairs.*)

BETSY. I saw them, I tell you. It was horrible.

JANE. Is my make-up all right?

HUGH. You look perfect.

JUSTIN. (*grabs a bottle from the bar*) We'll all have a stiff drink and forget this ever happened.

BETSY. (*as she goes off upstairs landing*) I never believed in ghosts.

VALERIE. I bet it was your imagination.

JANE. You lose your bet. (*They are off.*)

HUGH. (*at foot of stairs watching them go*) They're going to cover everything up. That's immoral.

JANE. You should talk. (*to KITTY*) Will you still get credit even if they aren't caught?

KITTY. They'll be caught all right. Wait till you see what I've got in here. (*rushes out to the library*)

HUGH. (*goes to JANE*) What's she up to?

JANE. Maybe we can bring disasters on them like making Valerie's next face lift a face drop.

KITTY. (*Enters with casette; she is munching a chocolate.*) I found another. A nougat.

JANE. That doesn't help us.

KITTY. But this does. (*holds up tape*)

HUGH. A casette.

KITTY. I put this on after Betsy fainted. It has the confession and all their plotting.

JANE. (*rises*) Kitty, you're a genius.

KITTY. The chocolates did it. If I hadn't gone back in there for them, I never would have thought to put on another casette.

JANE. You will get through the gates now, won't you?

KITTY. I've made it. I'll see you when you get in.

JANE. Will it be ages?

KITTY. Get to work on those demerits, stop people from sinning. Come on, Hugh, I'll drop you off at your waiting room after we leave this off with the police. (*crosses* D.R.) It'll save postage.

HUGH. (*goes to her*) Can I take a good book and a cushion with me?

KITTY. Haven't you heard, you can't take it with you.

HUGH. (*turns*) Goodbye, Jane. I really am sorry about—what happened.

JANE. (*crosses* C.) By the time you get through the gates, perhaps I'll have forgotten. Kitty, don't you want to clear out the refrigerator?

KITTY. Not now. I can eat gourmet for eternity. Hurry up, Hugh.

HUGH. Is my waiting room air conditioned? I'm feeling very warm.

KITTY. (*as she leads him off* D.R.) And you're going to feel a lot warmer before you're through.

JANE. But what about me? (*sits on sofa despondently*) How does one stop people from being naughty? Where do I find sinners? (*looks out at audience, does a take, looks again and slowly smiles*) Ohh, they're still here. They look like the type to put slugs in parking meters, and I bet they're forgetting to report everything on their income taxes. (*rises and walks down to audience*) How about you, sir? Is that your wife sitting next to you? And you—how about you—? (*The lights have dimmed to black and curtain.*)

PROPERTY LIST

ACT ONE

On Stage:
2 bowls of snacks, one of which is olives, scotch, brandy,
  vodka, etc. bottles, glasses both highball and loball
  size, ice bucket on bar
Bowl of waxed fruit with one apple on shelves
Hangers and coats in closet

Off Down Right (outside and kitchen):
Rule book with loose papers in it (KITTY)
Tray with demi-tasse (5), sugar and spoons (KITTY)
Banana (KITTY)

Off Down Left (Library):
Kleenex (EDWINA)

ACT TWO

Off Down Right (outside and kitchen):
Ice for bucket (KITTY)
Cookie (KITTY)

Off Down Left (Library):
Timer plug (KITTY)
Silencer (KITTY)
Paper with list written on it (EDWINA)
Casette (BETSY)
2 chocolates (KITTY)
Casette (KITTY)

Off Up Center (Upstairs):
8 × 10 photograph of VALERIE (VALERIE)

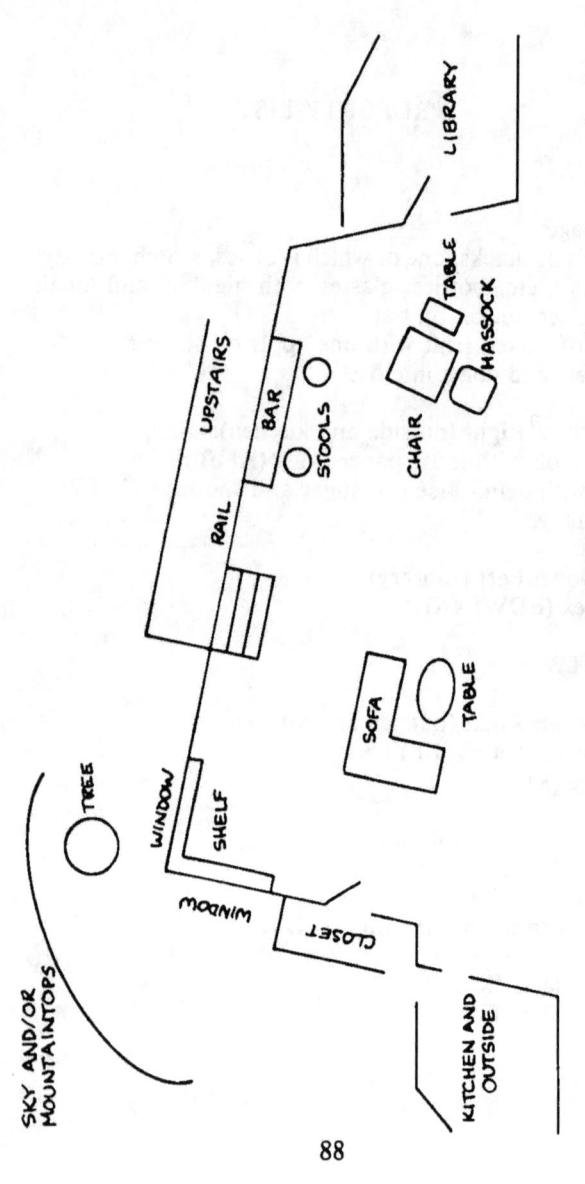

SCENE DESIGN
"MURDER ON THE RERUN"

88

MUSIC USE NOTE

Licensees are solely responsible for obtaining formal written permission from copyright owners to use copyrighted music in the performance of this play and are strongly cautioned to do so. If no such permission is obtained by the licensee, then the licensee must use only original music that the licensee owns and controls. Licensees are solely responsible and liable for all music clearances and shall indemnify the copyright owners of the play(s) and their licensing agent, Samuel French, against any costs, expenses, losses and liabilities arising from the use of music by licensees. Please contact the appropriate music licensing authority in your territory for the rights to any incidental music.

IMPORTANT BILLING AND CREDIT REQUIREMENTS

If you have obtained performance rights to this title, please refer to your licensing agreement for important billing and credit requirements.

www.ingramcontent.com/pod-product-compliance
Lightning Source LLC
Chambersburg PA
CBHW070639120726
47909CB00004B/1499

* 9 7 8 0 5 7 3 6 1 9 7 1 7 *